Simon lifted a hand and waved. Do they know that?" Lucien asked. "Because it looks like they want you to join them."

"Not me, Lucien," Tim said with a laugh. "Get over there."

Shock was like a punch to the stomach. Lucien blinked. "What?"

"You know how to play, right?" Tim asked, and on autopilot, Lucien nodded. "Great. It's just a friendly kick around, so you've got nothing to worry about. Go on, they're waiting."

Forcing his legs to move, Lucien crossed the space between him and Simon, who was grinning broadly.

"Are you crazy?" he asked, and his lover laughed.

"Maybe. But mostly I'm crazy about you. Come on, Luc—football is a huge part of my life. Let me share it with you."

Despite his better judgment, Lucien smiled. How could he say no to that?

WELCOME TO
 REAMSPUN DESIRES

Dear Reader,

Love is the dream. It dazzles us, makes us stronger, and brings us to our knees. Dreamspun Desires tell stories of love featuring your favorite heartwarming heroes, captivating plots, and exotic locations. Stories that make your breath catch and your imagination soar.

In the pages of these wonderful love stories, readers can escape to a world where love conquers all, the tenderness of a first kiss sweeps you away, and your heart pounds at the sight of the one you love.

When you put it all together, you find romance in its truest form.

Love always finds a way.

Elizabeth North

Executive Director
Dreamspinner Press

Louisa Masters

THE ATHLETE AND THE ARISTOCRAT

PUBLISHED BY

Published by
DREAMSPINNER PRESS

5032 Capital Circle SW, Suite 2, PMB# 279,
Tallahassee, FL 32305-7886 USA
www.dreamspinnerpress.com

This is a work of fiction. Names, characters, places, and incidents either are the product of author imagination or are used fictitiously, and any resemblance to actual persons, living or dead, business establishments, events, or locales is entirely coincidental.

The Athlete and the Aristocrat
© 2019 Louisa Masters.
Editorial Development by Sue Brown-Moore.

Cover Art
© 2019 Alexandria Corza.
http://www.seeingstatic.com/
Cover content is for illustrative purposes only and any person depicted on the cover is a model.

Paperback ISBN: 978-1-64108-107-8
Digital ISBN: 978-1-64080-778-5
Library of Congress Control Number: 2018907598
Paperback published January 2019
v. 1.0

Printed in the United States of America
∞
This paper meets the requirements of
ANSI/NISO Z39.48-1992 (Permanence of Paper).

LOUISA MASTERS started reading romance much earlier than her mother thought she should. While other teenagers were sneaking out of the house, Louisa was sneaking romance novels in and working out how to read them without being discovered. She's spent most of her life feeling sorry for people who don't read, convinced that books are the solution to every problem. As an adult, she feeds her addiction in every spare second, only occasionally tearing herself away to do things like answer the phone and pay bills. She spent years trying to build a "sensible" career, working in bookstores, recruitment, resource management, administration, and as a travel agent, before finally conceding defeat and devoting herself to the world of romance novels. Louisa has a long list of places first discovered in books that she wants to visit, and every so often she overcomes her loathing of jet lag and takes a trip that charges her imagination. She lives in Melbourne, Australia, where she whines about the weather for most of the year while secretly admitting she'll probably never move.

Website: www.louisamasters.com

Facebook: www.facebook.com/LouisaMastersAuthor

Email: louisa@louisamasters.com

By Louisa Masters

DREAMSPUN DESIRES
#43 – The Bunny and the Billionaire
#73 – The Athlete and the Aristocrat

Published by **DREAMSPINNER PRESS**
www.dreamspinnerpress.com

Becky Johnson is a legend. That's all.

Chapter One

NOT fidgeting was hard.

That's stupid, he told himself. He was *Simon Wood*, for fuck's sake, a championship professional athlete. He'd been in more high-pressure situations than most people would care to even imagine—on the pitch, in the locker room, in the media spotlight. He was used to being nervous, and not since he was nineteen had he felt the urge to fidget.

This was more important than anything else he'd done, however, although he'd never say so to the millions of football fans around the world, many of whom either idolized or loathed him. But it was. As much as he'd always loved playing football, his career as an athlete was never going to be forever, and while it brought entertainment and pleasure to many, ultimately that had been fleeting. This, though... this could last a long time and benefit a lot of young people.

So Si made a concerted effort not to tap his fingers on the chair arms as he sat in the executive reception of the Morel Corporation in Paris. It was a fantastic coup to have even gotten this appointment with Édouard Morel—most applications for charitable funds went through the Morel Foundation's director—but once Si had retired and made the decision that this was what he wanted to do next, he'd called in just about every favor he'd ever been owed and leaned on a few contacts he'd made in his playing years just to get this meeting. The Morel Corporation had been his top pick when he'd been compiling a list of possible backers because Édouard Morel was known for following through on promises to charities and for generosity. He needed the older man's full backing, including his contacts and influence, not just to be one of many charities on the Foundation's list.

"Monsieur Wood?" Si looked up as the extremely elegant executive receptionist came toward him, her professional smile just that tiny bit *more* than it should be. He was used to that, of course, from both women and men, and any other time he may have considered signaling that he was open to her offer, but not today. Not here. He would do nothing to bollocks up this meeting.

He kept his smile as neutral as possible as he stood. "Yes?"

"If you come this way, Monsieur Morel will see you now." Her manner slipped back to purely professional. His message had obviously been received.

Taking a deep breath and trying not to be obvious about it, Si followed her down a hallway. At the end was a set of double doors, and with each step closer, his heart pounded a tiny bit louder in his ears. *Relax, Si. You can do this.*

They reached the doors, and the woman—she'd told him her name earlier, but he couldn't for the life of him remember it—knocked once before opening one and poking her head in. A moment later she opened both doors wide and stepped back, motioning for him to enter.

"Thank you," he said, his throat suddenly dry, and walked past her. He heard the doors close behind him, but his focus was on the man rising from a fancy chair behind the big desk across the room. "Monsieur Morel, I'm so pleased to meet you," Si said as he crossed the space between them, hand outstretched. "I'm Simon Wood." He knew the man spoke English, which was a great relief since his French was not good and mainly limited to the sort of slurs that could be used against opponents during a football match.

"I recognize you," Édouard Morel replied, smiling broadly. "I am not so great a sports fan as my son, but even I could not fail to know who you are." He shook Si's hand and gestured for him to sit, while Si wondered if the comment about not being a great sports fan meant he was screwed.

Only one way to find out.

"I must confess, I am very curious about this new venture you wanted to speak about. I am not in the habit of funding new businesses, but several people insisted I must see you."

Oh, bloody hell. It sounded like Morel was setting up for a refusal already, and Si had only introduced himself!

"It's not exactly a new business," Si said, forcing the words through his suddenly too-tight throat. Morel raised an eyebrow, his expression skeptical... and just like that, Si was in his zone. The nerves fell away, the worry disappeared, and he was hyperfocused, completely intent on the end goal.

He knew he was speaking, knew he'd taken out the business plan and was making his presentation, but he wasn't sure exactly what he said. He felt confident, though, sure of every word and action, could judge Morel's reactions and change tack as required.

And those reactions weren't always positive. "*I do not spend charitable funds on games*," had very nearly pulled Si out of his focused state.

Finally he sat back in his chair, awareness widening again as Morel flipped once more through the business plan for the program. He'd made his pitch. Now to see if it had worked.

Morel looked up, and Si's gut clenched. "You have secured 25 percent of the funding required for startup and the first year?"

Si nodded. "Yes. There are various grant organizations across Europe that have indicated they would be happy to support the program. I can't officially apply for them until we're up and running, of course, but I've been assured the funds will be allocated when I do. That will account for 5 percent. The other twenty is coming from me."

Morel seemed impressed by that. "Really? Twenty percent?"

"I was very good at my job, monsieur, and not as foolish with money as some might assume footballers are. I strongly believe that this program can do a lot of good, and I'd be an idiot not to put my money where my mouth is before looking for funding." *Was that too aggressive?* Maybe he should have just shut up.

"Very well." Morel put the business plan down and sat back in his superfancy chair. "I will not lie—I have never been inclined to support sports charities. I believe

money is better used on basic necessities and education."
Si's stomach sank. "However, you have made a very
good point that sometimes young people have different
priorities and that life cannot just be about necessities.
Pleasure is important too. So here is what I propose.
You have 25 percent of funding already secured. The
Morel Corporation—not the Foundation—will fund an
additional 60 percent of what you need for the first five
years of the program, with an option to review then."

Si wanted to leap up and scream in victory. Sixty
percent was more—heaps more—than what he'd
hoped for from Morel, and a five-year commitment?
Outstanding! Instead, he smiled broadly. "That's very
generous of you, sir. Thank you. You won't regret this."

Morel held up a hand. "I am not finished. You have an
MBA and an excellent understanding of football and the
needs of young players, but I believe no actual experience
with running a business or charitable endeavor?"

Where's he going with this? "That's correct, sir, and
why the plan"—he nodded to the bound document on the
desk—"allows for the hire of an experienced business
manager."

"But surely those funds can be put to better use?
Let me instead propose this. My son, Lucien, will
consult on the setup of the program, train you to run it,
and oversee operations for the first five years. His time
and expertise will be an additional part of the Morel
Corporation's contribution."

There was a roaring sound in Si's ears. Morel was
giving him an executive consultant? Si couldn't claim
to be current on who all the movers and shakers of
the business world were, but Lucien Morel appeared
in the business news almost as often as his father.
Having his knowledge and expertise attached to the

program would be…. Si couldn't even think of a word to describe how good.

Belatedly, he realized Morel was still speaking.

"… and so I will personally provide the final 15 percent of funding that you require."

Si blinked. "I…. Sorry, could you repeat that?" He knew it was less than professional, but he needed to hear the words again.

Morel smiled. "I said, I am aware that it may prove difficult to obtain funding from other organizations with a Morel representative overseeing operations, so I will personally provide the additional funds. No insult to you, but with the size of the contribution the Morel Corporation is making, I would feel more comfortable to have Lucien involved, and if that requires an additional contribution from me…." He shrugged, a very Gallic gesture, and Si nodded. Christ, was it Christmas? His birthday? Every good day he'd ever experienced rolled into one? There could be no other explanation for the level of good fortune he was in receipt of today.

He stood when Morel did. "I will have Lucien's assistant contact you to arrange an appointment, but here is his information. His name is Paul." Si took the offered business card, feeling rather numb, shook the man's hand, and left the office. He walked down the hall, nodded to the receptionist, rode the lift down thirty floors, and left the building. It wasn't until he was out on the busy Paris street, faced with several hours before he needed to be at the airport for his flight home, that it hit him.

He'd done it.

Twenty years of wondering, of wishing, of thinking maybe one day. The scrupulous efforts to put money aside during his early playing days, when teammates his age were blowing thousands—sometimes millions—

on posh houses and cars, holidays abroad, and designer gear. The years of scraping out time to study for his degrees in addition to his grueling training, match, and publicity schedules.

It was all paying off. He'd had the business plan, and now he had the funding too.

And an executive consultant of the like he could never have dreamed of hiring.

Si laughed out loud as he walked down the street, everything seeming bolder, brighter, happier.

He loved Paris.

Chapter Two

Four months later

LUCIEN hated London.

He'd always hated it. Tourists to Europe seemed to love it, and he'd even heard some of his friends speak fondly of it, but for Lucien, London was hell.

He hated the weather. He hated the congested streets and the masses of tourists. He hated that he felt stupid for hating the traffic and tourists because he lived in Paris, and it wasn't any better there. But somehow, in London these things annoyed him more.

And most of all, he hated the English, which led to more self-hatred, because a Frenchman hating the English was so stereotypical it was laughable, and Lucien hated to be laughed at. Laughed with, certainly—he was considered the "fun" one among his friends—but not at. Yet he deserved to be laughed at for hating London—it was a childish, stupid thing, the remnants of a long-ago embarrassment that left a lingering bad feeling. He couldn't even remember for certain what had embarrassed him, only that it had happened in London. Through the rain-splattered tinted window of the car, he glared at the backed-up traffic and crowds of people who didn't even have the sense to get out of the rain. He had one more meeting, just one, and then he'd be on a plane and heading back to Paris. Tomorrow he would be in Monaco for the weekend, visiting his best friends and relaxing, away from the stress of business. Perhaps he'd change his plans and fly directly to Monaco today. But first, he had to make it through a few more hours of London.

He leaned forward to speak to his driver. "How long will it take to get there?" he asked politely. It was the same man who always drove him in London, but Lucien didn't know his name. His friend Ben would probably give him a reproachful look if he ever found that out, and Lucien pushed aside a pang of guilt. He'd never thought about things like drivers' names before he'd met Ben.

The man half turned to look at Lucien. "Sorry, sir, it'll be at least another half hour. The rain always makes the traffic worse." It took Lucien a moment to decipher the words. His English had improved a lot since Ben had come into his life, but he was now used to English spoken with an Australian accent, and the myriad of varied British accents had always confounded him anyway.

"Thank you," he said, leaning back again. It would probably be faster if he walked, but then he'd be one of those idiots without the sense to get out of the rain. He sighed and pulled out his laptop. Since he probably wasn't going to have time for a briefing before the meeting, he'd have to check the notes his assistant always emailed him.

Lucien read the first paragraph, blinked, then read it again. And again. Was this a joke? Was Paul so sick of sending him notes he didn't read that he'd decided to send him fiction instead?

Or was he actually going to be meeting with one of the twenty-first century's best football players to date, and helping the man set up a football scholarship program?

Wouldn't he have heard about it if such a program had been in the works? The corporation belonged to his family, after all. Lucien's official title may have been Executive Consultant, but that was only because his father wanted him to obtain expertise in all branches of business, across all the companies under the corporate umbrella. Eventually, he'd be the CEO, and his father had always insisted he be fully aware of everything going on within the corporation. A program like this, and especially if he would be involved in setting it up, was something he should have known about.

He pulled out his phone and tapped in a speed-dial code, then skimmed through the rest of the document as he waited for the call to connect.

"Lucien?" his assistant, Paul, asked. Lucien didn't bother with pleasantries.

"What's this scholarship program?" There was a momentary hesitation, which surprised Lucien. He knew Paul would know what he was talking about— the man memorized Lucien's calendar and personally prepared the information Lucien would need.

"Your father didn't tell you?" Paul asked slowly, and Lucien closed his eyes. The last time his father had communicated directly with Paul and not told Lucien about it, Lucien had ended up in Helsinki for a month in the middle of winter. The Finns were wonderful people, but their country was damn cold in February.

"No," he said, trying not to snap. This was not Paul's fault, but Lucien was going to insist that he immediately report any future interaction he had with Lucien's father.

"Oh. Well, after his retirement last year, Simon Wood approached your father. He had a fairly detailed business plan—which I haven't seen but thought your father would give you a copy of—and your father was impressed by his proposal. He agreed, but stipulated that the setup and first five years of the program would need to be supervised by you. The idea is to provide funding for training, equipment, transport, anything needed for children in Europe aged between seven and eighteen who show talent for football but might be prevented from playing for financial reasons. I believe there was also something about summer training camps. It's all nonprofit, of course, and your father agreed that the Morel Corporation would fund 60 percent of the program. Wood is putting up 20 percent himself"— Lucien blinked. *Really?*—"and has found several grants across Europe to cover approximately another 5 percent. Your father indicated that the remainder of the funds would come from him personally."

That was another shock. His father had always insisted that lack of philanthropy contributed to most of the world's problems, and that he would never put himself in a position to be accused of ignoring the plight of those less fortunate. As a result, employees of the Morel Corporation received pay and benefits in the top 3-percent bracket of the EU, and both the Corporation and the Morel family personally donated hundreds of millions every year, most through the Morel Foundation, but also through other organizations. However, his father usually eschewed what he termed "frivolous" charities. Food, shelter, health, and education were his favorites. He would occasionally donate to environmental causes, but something to encourage recreational sport? Before today Lucien would have said it would never happen.

As to Simon Wood funding 20 percent himself… well, that was a surprise also. Yes, he had been one of the top-earning footballers in the world until his retirement, with endorsement deals aplenty also, but to be able to put up that kind of cash money, he must have an excellent financial manager.

Lucien thanked Paul and ended the call, reading the provided information again and making notes for himself. He pushed down the thrill of excitement that crept through him. This program was the kind of thing he'd always wanted to get started but hadn't because of time constraints and parental expectations. He'd always been a huge football fan, went to as many matches as he could and watched the rest on TV, but aside from casual matches with friends as a teenager or school sports, he'd never played. His father hadn't approved, insisting he had other responsibilities.

The last page of Paul's notes was a profile of Simon Wood, and this time Lucien couldn't stop the zing that shot through him. Simon Wood, age thirty-four, retired championship footballer. There was a list of his charitable endeavors, and a paragraph about his schooling—apparently the man had found time somewhere in his career to get an MBA—but nowhere had Paul included one very important fact: Simon Wood was hot.

Ridiculously hot.

So hot that he'd consistently made hottest bachelor lists around the world over the last decade.

He was also rumored to be bisexual. There had never been any confirmation, not even a tell-all tabloid story, but the gossip mill murmured that while Simon publicly only had girlfriends, his bed was not restricted to a single gender. When Lucien had been a horny fourteen-year-old struggling to understand his own sexuality, the rumors about then-nineteen-year-old football sensation Simon Wood had grounded him and helped him get his head around exactly why he could be turned on by both Jennifer Lopez *and* Hugh Jackman.

Not to mention, the man himself had played a starring role in many of Lucien's teenage fantasies.

Just the sound of his name was sexy... *Sigh*-mon. And he was so utterly sigh-worthy.

His phone dinged, saving him from what had the potential to become a *very* uncomfortable moment, what with his driver being in the car. He glanced at the screen and smiled.

Are you still coming for a long weekend? Léo suggested dinner at Le Louis XV, and I need to make a reservation.

Ben's obsession with reservations was a hangover from the days before he'd inherited millions and moved to Monaco to live with his French billionaire boyfriend—and something that still vaguely puzzled Lucien. He'd never really thought about letting a restaurant know he was coming before Ben had made a big deal about it. He wanted to eat, he picked a place, they found a table for him. Admittedly it would be terrible if people had been inconvenienced for his sake, but that probably didn't happen. Or the restaurant would make it worth their while if it did.

Right?

He texted back in French, confirming his plans and adding that he might arrive that evening. After a lot of humorous and sometimes ridiculous miscommunication, he and Ben had agreed that Ben would send texts written only in English, and Lucien would send texts written only in French. Although they were both fairly fluent speakers of each language, their literacy was not so good. No text-speak was to be used, only proper words and sentences. That way, they could both practice reading each other's language. Léo, Ben's boyfriend and one of Lucien's best friends, who had often been called on to decipher or interpret their texts before the agreement, had opened a bottle of champagne to celebrate when he heard.

Awesome. Let us know when you get in.

Deciding that there was no reason to spend the night in Paris, Lucien texted his pilot with his amended destination. He was still smiling at the thought of seeing his friends and *getting out of London* when the car finally pulled up in front of the Morel Corporation London building. He slipped the laptop back into its bag as his driver got out and opened the door for him.

"Thank you," he murmured. He wasn't sure what the driver—or any of his drivers, for that matter—did while he was in meetings, but the man was always waiting for him when he was done. Probably some secretary called him and told him Lucien was on the way. As he strode into the building, Lucien wondered vaguely if the secretary would include that as a skill on their résumé: punctually informs drivers of—

He shook his head, inwardly cursing Ben. He'd never used to think about things like that. Before he met Ben, drivers could have appeared by magic for all he knew and cared.

He was met at the elevator by Margot, the senior assistant to the Director of UK Operations, who was usually seconded to him when he was in London.

"Traffic?" she asked briskly, hitting the call button for the elevator. She was an extremely efficient, no-nonsense woman in her forties, and Lucien had the impression that if she had been in the car with him, the traffic would not have dared delay them. She reminded him somewhat of his mother, only her suit wasn't high-end designer.

"Yes" was all he responded. She wouldn't have tolerated chitchat.

"Your meeting is here already. He has coffee and hasn't complained about the delay."

Lucien shot her a surprised glance as they stepped into the elevator and she pressed the button for the top floor. He was Lucien Morel. People waited for him, and if they complained, they were shown the door. Most didn't use it, because he was Lucien Morel and an appointment with him was hard to get and not taken lightly.

Margot's cheeks were slightly pink, and she carefully studied the floor. Lucien grinned. "Are you a football fan, Margot?" he asked, breaking the unspoken business-only policy between them.

The pink darkened. "Not really," she said stiffly, and Lucien laughed.

"Ah, a footballer fan, then." The outraged look she shot him was tinged with embarrassment. "Don't worry, you are not the only one."

The elevator doors opened, and he walked out wondering if he'd regret that comment.

WHEN Lucien entered the meeting room that had been allocated for his use while he was in London, he found Simon Wood sitting at the table working on a laptop. The man was so involved in what he was doing that he didn't look up, and Lucien took the opportunity to study him.

Lust kicked in his gut.

He'd never met Wood in person before, and that was a damn shame, because television and photos didn't do him justice. The black hair was cut short, but still thick and silky-looking. His jaw and cheekbones could have been chiseled by a master sculptor, and his skin lacked the pallor many of the English had—probably due to hours spent outside on the football pitch. He was wearing a tailored shirt, open at the collar, and Lucien's gaze followed the line of that throat down to where a light smattering of hair was visible….

He swallowed. *Focus, Lucien!* He could not allow himself to be distracted. A project like this was something he'd always dreamed of, and if he wanted to convince his father to support similar ones in the future, it had to be a runaway success.

He cleared his throat and closed the door behind him. Wood looked up and smiled, and Lucien was glad he still had his hand on the doorknob, because his knees may have gone a little weak.

"Lucien Morel?" Wood asked, standing, and Lucien let go of the doorknob and crossed to the table, reaching out to shake the other man's hand.

"Yes. A pleasure, Mr. Wood. I'm a big fan." He forced the words through his suddenly too-narrow throat and wondered what the hell was wrong with him. Even as a teenager, he'd always been confident.

"Simon, please. We're probably going to be spending a lot of time on this, and I'm not really good with formality."

"Lucien," Lucien offered, convinced he must be going insane because for some reason Simon Wood's accent was turning him on.

Turning.

Him.

On.

He pulled out a chair and sat a bit hurriedly. A British accent, turning him on. He needed to get the hell out of England.

Wood—Simon—resumed his seat. "So, Lucien, what do you think of this project? Your father gave me the impression that you were pretty excited about it. I know I am. I'm looking forward to hearing your thoughts on the plan—you have so much more experience in this than I do."

Damn. Lucien inwardly cursed his father. He hated looking foolish.

"My father was right—I'm definitely excited." He forced himself to ignore the unintended double entendre. "This is the kind of project I've been wanting to be part of for a long time." There, that was safe. "But my father neglected to pass on a copy of the business plan. Do you have one here? We should go through it together." That was reasonable, and no need to mention that he'd had no idea about the program until half an hour ago.

Except the look Simon gave him was somehow both surprised and disappointed, and Lucien felt like a schoolboy being called on the carpet. Clearly Simon thought Lucien hadn't been bothered to prepare for the meeting.

Simon opened a manila folder that was sitting next to his laptop and pulled out a bound document. He passed it across the table without comment.

"Thank you," Lucien said, then in an attempt to regain control of the situation, and perhaps wipe that look from Simon's face, he added, "Tell me, what inspired this program for you?" He flipped open the document and began to scan the summary. He knew, after years of experience reading such documents, exactly which sections he needed to look at for the kind of preliminary planning they would do today. He turned a page, and realized that Simon was silent.

Lucien glanced up. "You don't want to tell me what inspired the program?" he asked, then wondered if that sounded snotty. Ben had told him that sometimes he came across as autocratic. Lucien had initially taken it as a compliment until Ben and a wincing Léo had explained it was not.

From the expression on Simon's face, he agreed with Ben.

"You're busy reading" was all he said, and his tone was no longer friendly. Lucien wished for what seemed like the millionth time that he was away from London. How could meeting a man who had always been an idol to him for the purpose of establishing a charity to assist underprivileged children to play football have become such a disaster?

He sighed. His hand itched to rub his forehead, but that type of gesture had been groomed out of him by first his nanny and then the teachers at the exclusive private schools he'd attended.

Lucien decided that blunt honesty was probably a better option than business diplomacy. Simon Wood had always been fairly forthright in media interviews, and if they were going to be working on this program together for at least five years, they definitely didn't want to start on the wrong foot.

"Simon, I'm sorry. The truth is, my father neglected to tell me about this program. I am not sure why; perhaps he just overlooked it. I first heard about it in the car on the way here. I *am* excited about it, though. It is the sort of project I have always wanted to be part of, and I am eager to see what you have in mind." He smiled the social, charming smile that had served him so well over the years, and was heartened when the set look on Simon's face softened a little, even if he didn't smile back. "Please tell me what inspired this program. I promise, I can listen and read. I have had a lot of practice." He increased the sincerity behind his smile.

Simon snorted. "All right, mate, ease up. I get it, you care, even if you've got no idea what's happening. Go on, start reading."

For a moment, Lucien floundered, taken aback. Then Simon grinned at him, and he tightened his grip on the business plan.

He smiled back weakly, and dropped his gaze to the page he'd been reading.

"So, I started playing football when I was a kid. Always loved it, always knew I was good at it," Simon said, not boastfully, just factually. "And I was lucky because my parents could manage the cost of all the gear and the club fees. Football kept me busy, and it kept me out of trouble. But I had this mate who played with me for years. He was good too, and it was pretty much known that the two of us were probably going to go on to play professionally." He paused as Lucien turned a page, and when Lucien glanced up, he continued. "When we were about thirteen, his parents split up. Well, his dad just split, really, took off and was never heard from again. His mum had only ever been a housewife, and suddenly she had to go out and find a job to support herself and three kids. She wasn't qualified for much, so money got tight, and they had to cut back on luxuries—like football."

Lucien winced even as he skimmed another page. He'd never had to worry about money, but it was obvious where this story was going.

"Jack—my mate—had a lot of trouble adjusting. They had to move to a council estate, he changed schools, and the only time he got to play football was at his new school, with kids he didn't know, who weren't serious about it. He got caught up in a new crowd, a rough crowd, stopped answering when I called. About six months after I saw him last, just a few days after he would have turned fifteen, there was an article in the local paper about him. He died of a heroin overdose."

Lucien put the business plan down. "I'm so sorry," he said softly. He'd seen the damage drugs could do in any social circle.

Simon shrugged. "It was rough. He'd been so dedicated to his sport, and he was a good mate. I couldn't help thinking that if he'd been able to keep playing, it might have been different. Even at a different school, he'd still have had all his football mates, and a lot of his time would have been taken with training. Maybe things would still have turned out the way they did, but…." He shrugged again. "Who knows? It just made me think about how unfair it is that so many kids have the ability and the drive, but are held back because of money, especially in some of the poorer countries."

Looking back at the plan, Lucien turned that over in his head. Yes, nobody could know whether Jack would have gotten into drugs or not if he'd still been playing football, but the truth was, it could be an expensive game. Not for kids playing in the park, but any who wanted to forge a career in it needed to consider club fees, gear, training camps… and the costs could be prohibitive for low- or even middle-income families. It was one of the reasons he'd always wanted to start a program like this.

He pulled out his laptop and logged in. "This is what I am thinking," he said, and Simon smiled.

TWO hours later, Lucien stretched. His back had been screaming for attention for far too long, but he hadn't wanted to break the flow of progress to move. He looked at his watch and winced. "I've kept you far longer than I should have," he apologized to Simon, who shook his head.

"Nah, it's not a problem. This program is my life priority right now." The man was keenly intelligent, and had eaten up everything Lucien had to say, often taking information and coming up with new ideas on the spot. They had pages of notes, and a rough plan for moving forward.

"If you don't have any other appointments to go to, perhaps we can continue. I'd like to finish drafting the—" Lucien broke off as someone knocked. "Enter."

The door opened, and Margot stuck her head in. "Apologies, but your pilot has called. With the weather worsening, he's afraid they may close the executive airport later today. He's managed to secure a departure slot for ninety minutes from now, but if you're going to make it, you'll need to leave soon." Lucien looked at his watch again. He really did not want to be stuck in London another night, but he would have liked to continue for at least a few more hours.

He looked at Simon speculatively. "How serious were you about this program being your 'life priority'?" he asked. Simon raised an eyebrow.

"Completely," he assured, and Lucien smiled.

"Excellent. Why don't you come with me? We can get quite a bit more done in transit, and then this evening."

Simon shrugged. "Sure. I can come back in the morning, I guess. It's not like Paris to London is a long flight."

Lucien, midway through packing up his laptop, stopped as he remembered. "Oh—I'm not going to Paris. I'm going to Monaco. Is that all right?"

"Monaco?" Simon shrugged again. "Sure. Haven't been there for a while. Maybe I'll stay the weekend. The weather's better than here."

"The weather is better than here *anywhere*," Lucien said, then paused. "Except Helsinki in February. I would prefer London at any time to Helsinki in February."

Simon quirked an eyebrow. "Sounds like there's a story there."

Slinging his laptop bag over his shoulder, Lucien led the way out the door and toward the elevator. "Not a story. A February in Helsinki."

With a snort Simon jabbed the call button for the elevator as Margot glided over. "Your car is downstairs," she informed Lucien, "and the pilot is standing by. He's filed a flight plan for Nice, and a car will meet you at the airport. I let Paul know you weren't coming back to Paris, and he said he's emailed you a list of things that need your attention today. Is there anything else I can do for you?"

"Nothing, thank you— Oh." Lucien turned to Simon. "Do you mind staying at my apartment this evening? There are rooms to choose from, but if you prefer a hotel—"

Simon was already shaking his head. "Your place is fine. Thanks for the offer." He smiled warmly, and for a moment, Lucien forgot where he was.

"Yes. Fine. Thank you, Margot. Would you please call the concierge at my apartment building in Monaco and have him arrange for some overnight things for Mr. Wood?"

"Oh, that's not necessary," Simon protested, but Margot just smiled and said, "Of course. Do you have any preferences, Mr. Wood?"

The elevator doors opened just then, and Lucien stepped inside as Simon insisted he could make do. Margot nodded and kept smiling, and Simon seemed to come to the realization that he wasn't going to win. "Thank you," he told her, and got in the elevator.

Lucien hit the button for the lobby and nodded to Margot as the doors closed.

"It really isn't necessary, you know," Simon said stubbornly. "It's only one night. I could have made do."

Lucien looked at him in surprise. "But why should you have to?" he asked, genuinely confused. Was this a British thing? "You are my guest, and I would be a very bad host if I didn't see to your needs." He jerked his gaze away as he realized what he'd said, and hoped Simon didn't think he'd meant the double entendre. *This is ridiculous*, he thought. *Why am I acting like a scared virgin?*

As the elevator doors opened, he directed the conversation back to the program, and soon they were ensconced in the back of his car, only slightly damp from their dash through the rain, discussing the pros and cons of various selection criteria as they were whisked to the executive airport.

Chapter Three

SI settled into the plush seat on the private plane, drink in hand, and tried not to be impressed. He wasn't exactly hurting for cash himself, but the level of wealth Lucien Morel treated so casually was on a completely different playing field.

Fancy sending the concierge out for "overnight things"—what were "overnight things," anyway?—when he'd only be there one night. He could've slept starkers—he did most of the time anyway except for the winter—and his clothes would've been fine for tomorrow. It wasn't like he'd worked up a sweat today, sitting in a posh conference room *talking*.

Unbidden, the image of working up a sweat with Lucien popped into his mind, and he enjoyed it only for a moment before firmly pushing it aside. As delicious as Lucien was—he'd always liked blond men—there was no way he'd risk this program, not after Édouard Morel's initial skepticism about supporting a charity for "games." Si had at first considered the insistence that so important a personage as the Morel heir be attached to the project meant that Morel was serious in his backing, but then Lucien hadn't known anything about it.

Still, he knew now, and he'd been very enthusiastic. It was a blessing to have somebody with so much business experience to lend a hand, because while Si knew he was no dunce, he'd been focused on football for most of his life, and the theory involved in his degrees plus the limited experience he had looking after his own interests wouldn't get him far with this project.

Lucien came back from conferring with the pilot, and sank into the seat beside him. "It won't be long," he assured, and Si let the accented words wash over him. Lucien spoke great English, and was very easy to understand, which was a relief, because Si's French was truly limited. If he was going to be working with people all over Europe, he should probably look into learning at least a few key phrases from the most common languages.

He turned to Lucien to ask if he thought it would be worth the time, and saw him smiling at his phone. "Good news?" he asked.

Lucien looked up, still smiling, and he was so good-looking and charming that Si had to shift in his seat to ease a growing problem. "A friend," Lucien said. "I texted to let them know I would be in Monaco for breakfast tomorrow, and now Ben is being...." He frowned. "Cheeky?"

Was he asking if that was the right word? "That depends," Si said, "on what he said."

Lucien offered the phone, and Si took it and glanced at the open text string on the screen. Of the most recent two, the one Lucien had sent was in French, which Si didn't have a prayer of reading, but the last one was in English.

You're flying down before breakfast? That's not like you. Oh—one-night stand whose bed you want to escape from? :-P

Si grinned. "Definitely cheeky," he affirmed. "You didn't tell him you're flying in tonight?" He passed back the phone, and Lucien glanced again at the screen and shook his head.

"No. He will want me to join them this evening." He began tapping at the screen, but Si reached out and stayed him.

"Wait, I don't want to disrupt an evening you were going to spend with friends," he protested, but Lucien only smiled.

"There was no plan to do so. I wasn't supposed to fly in until tomorrow, so they were not even expecting me until late in the morning." He looked up and met Si's gaze. "Although, if you like I can tell them to join us later for a drink. I think you may even have met Malik once or twice before."

Malik? A jolt went through Si. "Malik al-Saud?" he asked. He was pretty sure that was the only Malik he'd ever met, back in his younger—and wilder—party days. The days he sometimes wished he could forget. The gleam in Lucien's eyes indicated this was probably one of those times.

"Yes, Malik al-Saud," he confirmed, and Si fought down panic as he remembered some of the very irresponsible things he'd done at a party where Malik had been in attendance.

"We've met," he said weakly. "Er—Lucien, I know you and your father are putting a lot of trust in me with this program, and I want you to know—"

"Relax." Lucien was outright grinning now, and once again it completely changed his handsome face. Where before he'd looked very autocratic, he now had a fun-loving air that made him all the more appealing. "I would never judge your current capacity for responsibility on past misdeeds. Malik himself no longer behaves in that way either. We must all grow up, yes?"

Relief made him laugh. "Yes," he agreed. "And yes, I remember Malik. We even had a few sober conversations. Sure, I'd like to see him again, and meet your cheeky friend."

Lucien went back to texting. "Ben—my cheeky friend—lives with Malik's cousin Léo. That's how I met him." He put his phone away as the plane jolted. "Now, you realize we will have to name this program?"

SI heard the front door buzzer go just as he finished washing his hands, and he braced himself to meet Lucien's friends. The afternoon and evening had been mentally exhausting, and he wished he hadn't encouraged Lucien to invite his friends around. He'd much prefer an early night. *And a couple more hours chatting with a sexy blond. Who're you kidding, old man? You just don't want to share.*

Shaking the thought away, Si examined himself in the mirror. He looked a bit tired, but considering he'd hardly slept for nerves last night, that was no surprise. And hadn't he felt like a right twat about that, considering he'd played hundreds of football matches in front of packed stadiums, some of them for championships, and not felt nervous about it since he was a teenager. But this program was important to him, and he'd been worried that the Morel heir would try to shunt him into a minor role. That seemed a stupid thought now—Lucien had made it very clear in his planning that Si would be taking on the lion's share of work, which made sense, really, since Lucien himself had a full-time job doing... whatever he did at the Morel Corporation.

Through the flight, the chauffeur-driven journey from Nice airport to the Morel family apartment on Avenue Princesse Grace, and the catered dinner Lucien had ordered, they'd worked. Si had vague memories of Malik al-Saud being a shiftless trust-fund baby, wandering from party to party, but that didn't seem to be the case with Lucien. The man had fielded emails and text messages while speaking to Si and fleshing the business plan out into a concrete step-by-step to-do list, complete with names of people to contact who might be able to assist. The only thing he hadn't done was take phone calls—every time the phone had rung, he'd sent it to voicemail. When Si had mentioned he didn't mind if Lucien took some calls, the blond had shaken his head. "Most of the time, it only needs to be a message, anyway," he'd said. "Anything urgent would be directed to my assistant, and I always answer his calls."

As a result, Si's dream of a football scholarship program to span Europe now had a solid foundation. He couldn't wait for Monday morning, when he could start setting their plans into motion. With luck, they'd be able to start sponsoring for next season.

First, though, he had to leave the bathroom and be social for a while. Come to think, wasn't Malik al-Saud the son of a royal? And his cousin, who was reportedly attached to him at the hip but whom Si had never met, was the son of another wealthy old French family. Contacts like that could only be good, right?

Mind made up, he left the bathroom and walked down the hall to the lavish living room they'd been working in. He heard voices, cheerful ones, babbling away in French, and grimaced. *Must learn language,* he reminded himself. If his association with the Morel Corporation was going to be a long and fruitful one, he should show that he valued it.

He walked into the living room, and conversation stopped. The three newcomers stared at him, two with surprise, but the gangly younger one looked more curious than anything else. Lucien wore a smug little smile.

"Hello," Si said, putting on his sponsorship smile. "I'm—"

"Simon Wood," Malik al-Saud said, coming forward with his hand outstretched and a wicked grin. "We've met before."

"I remember," Si said ruefully, shaking his hand. "Although I was almost hoping you'd forgotten."

Malik laughed. "We've all felt that way about something," he said. "Let's just leave the past alone, shall we?"

"Good plan," Si agreed, and even though Lucien had already said he wouldn't blame Si for his past peccadilloes, he felt immense relief.

"Simon Wood?" the gangly man said. "That sounds familiar." Si was surprised to note that the man spoke with an Australian accent. He studied Si, and then looked at Lucien. "I should recognize that name, shouldn't I? Have you told me about Simon before?"

The other three men shouted with laughter, and the Aussie flushed. "Crap, what have I said now?" He grimaced apologetically at Si. "If I've offended you, I'm really sorry."

"No offense, mate," Si assured him, wondering who this guy was, exactly. Possibly the Ben Lucien had spoken of earlier?

"Ben," the third man, tall, dark, and definitely worth a second look, said, confirming Si's guess, "Simon Wood is one of England's most successful football players."

"Was," Si corrected. He'd retired, hadn't he, and as much as he loved the sport, it had been a relief to pass the torch to the younger players.

"Football?" Ben asked. "Oh, right—soccer. Well, sorry, I might have heard your name somewhere, but that's about all I know about the sport. Congratulations on being so good?"

"Thanks," Si said, grinning. "Sorry, you're…?"

"Right, sorry." Ben shook his head and stepped forward, offering a hand. "Ben Adams." Si shook his hand, a little surprised by how firm his grip was. Looking at the man more closely, he saw that despite the gangly appearance, Ben actually had quite a lot of muscle.

"Nice to meet you," Si told him, genuinely meaning it. As the other man, the only one Si hadn't been introduced to, but who was presumably Malik's cousin, came forward, Ben turned his head and said, "You're supposed to keep me from making an idiot of myself, remember? That was the deal."

The man smiled, slid one arm around Ben's waist, and offered Si his other hand. "Léo Artois," he introduced himself. "A pleasure to meet you at last. I always regretted not going with Malik on that trip, but family…." He grimaced and shrugged, and Si laughed.

"If you'd been there too, I'd really be sweating now," he admitted, lulled by everyone's genuine friendliness. "I'm trying to be responsible these days."

"Yes, Lucien was just telling us about the program," Léo said, drawing Ben over to one of the sofas and sitting. Simon followed, and settled in a chair. "But he didn't mention that you were the person he was working with, or that you were here."

Si felt a sudden stab of alarm. Crap, was he intruding? "I'm sorry, I didn't mean to crash your—"

"You're not," Ben interrupted forcefully. "He meant that literally, that we didn't know you were here, not that we thought you shouldn't be." He jabbed his boyfriend in the ribs with an elbow.

"Indeed," Léo said, rubbing his side. "I misspoke. I am actually very pleased you are here. I have been a fan for years, though perhaps not so big a one as Lucien."

Lucien, in the process of pouring martinis, clanked the pitcher loudly against a glass, and all heads turned in his direction. Si was glad of the sudden reprieve. Lucien was a fan? Now that Si thought about it, both Lucien and his father had mentioned that, and it had been clear while they were working that Lucien followed football, knew the game well and many of the major stakeholders, but Si had somehow equated that to him being a football fan, not a fan of him, personally.

The idea made him feel... funny. Good funny.

Who was he kidding? It turned him way the hell on.

"Simon and I have been working on the program," Lucien said, and he sounded a little stiff. "He is staying here tonight and going back to London tomorrow. Unless...." He looked at Si, who felt the impact of that blue gaze like a punch to the gut. *He's a fan. Of me.* "You mentioned you might stay the weekend?"

Si forced himself to pull it together. "Er, I hadn't decided. It'd be nice to escape London and the rain for a bit, but I suppose it also depends if I can get a hotel—I forgot that it was so close to the Grand Prix, and hotels usually book up around now, don't they?" There, that was a fairly sensible answer. It in no way implied that he wanted Lucien to be one of the fanboys who'd slipped phone numbers to him, willing to sneak around for a night with a famous footballer.

Even if the idea was appealing.

"You are most welcome to stay here," Lucien said. "I would not dream of making you find a hotel."

"Oh, I couldn't—" Si began, because if *one* night in the man's apartment was already stirring up naughty thoughts, how much worse would two be?

"Don't be silly," Ben broke in. Si looked his way, and saw that Malik was leaning over the back of the sofa, grinning smugly. "He's got way too much space here anyway. Did you happen to count the bedrooms? Besides, Léo and I were in London last week, and the weather's total shit right now. You should definitely stay and enjoy the sunshine while you can. You'll probably be really busy with this program soon, right?"

"And this would give you the opportunity to do some more work," Malik interjected smoothly. "Lucien doesn't get to London often because he considers it akin to hell, so either you'll travel a lot yourself, video conference, or you could take advantage of the fact that his bedroom is right down the hall from yours."

Léo coughed, and Ben went red, and Si got the sneaking suspicion that while he and Lucien had been talking, the three of them had hatched some sort of nefarious plan. A quick glance at Lucien's set face seemed to indicate that he wasn't wrong. Since he wasn't averse to the idea of sneaking into Lucien's room, he pretended he'd missed the giant hint. "Perhaps Lucien doesn't want to spend the weekend working," he protested. "After all, he's here to visit with you."

Malik waved a hand and straightened. "So you come along, and we all talk business together. He was going to bring Léo into it all, anyway. I like football, and Ben likes meeting new people"—Léo choked on his martini—"and he's a nurse, so he can probably advise on injury management." Ben shot Malik a doubting look, but the other man had picked up his own glass and was taking a healthy swig.

"I was going to ask Léo to get involved," Lucien admitted, handing Si a glass. Si lifted it to his mouth, trying not to look like he was as desperate for the alcohol as he was. Seriously, he needed to get a grip. "He's the financial advisor I mentioned earlier today."

Si regarded Léo with new interest. Although they'd never met, the tales of the two cousins, Malik and Léo, were rather legendary on the party circuit. He'd never heard anything to indicate that Léo Artois was actually a genius financial advisor of the standard Lucien had spoken of.

"And it's right up his alley. He mostly does work for charities," Ben added. Léo shrugged.

"Well, maybe I will stay," Si said, trying to sound like he was conceding and not like he wanted to jump Lucien at the earliest opportunity. He didn't even know that the man was gay, although based on the heavy-handed hints his friends were dropping, it seemed likely. Plus, that zing every time they accidentally touched couldn't be just on his side, could it?

"Excellent," Malik pronounced. "We'll have plenty of time to talk business, I assure you. Our plans are quite loose—drinks tonight, breakfast and dinner tomorrow—"

"Dinner!" Ben exclaimed. "I should call and adjust the reservation."

Lucien laughed, Malik groaned, and Léo put his arm around Ben. Si frowned. "I don't want to cause any hassle—"

"Don't worry, Simon," Lucien said, "you won't be causing any hassle."

"Ben." Léo leaned toward his boyfriend, who was tapping the screen of his phone. "We've been through this before. Do you really think the restaurant is going to mind if we arrive with one extra person? They already know we're coming, thanks to your reservation." Ben had a particularly stubborn look on his face, and he slid out from under Léo's arm and stood.

"It will only take me a moment to call them," he insisted, and lifted his phone to his ear as he walked toward through french doors to the balcony. Léo sighed and leaned back.

"I feel as though I've missed something," Si admitted.

"Ben feels strongly that reservations are always required," Malik said, refilling his glass from the pitcher. "He gets… er, annoyed when we don't plan ahead."

Si nodded. Over the years, he'd taken advantage of the fact that his fame opened all manner of doors for him, which meant he could walk into almost any restaurant at any time and get a table. While he'd enjoyed it at first, it had made him rather uncomfortable after a while, especially when he remembered how long people waited for reservations at some of those restaurants. In the end, he'd compromised by calling ahead for a reservation if he knew what his plans were going to be, giving the restaurant time to rearrange things if necessary.

"That's very considerate of him," he said, just as Ben came back into the room.

"It's all sorted," he said, an edge of triumph in his voice, and Lucien laughed again.

"Come here," Léo demanded, grinning, and Ben went over and snuggled up next to him.

Chapter Four

LUCIEN was going to kill his friends.

It normally took a lot to embarrass him. He had a thick skin, hardened further by years in the business world, and he'd learned to shake off slights and disappointments. More, he'd always delighted in good-naturedly taunting his friends, and expected their retaliation. Just a month ago, Ben had viciously set him up on a date with a strict vegan. Lucien was not usually bothered by lifestyle choices, but that woman had been of the belief that all meat eaters were murderers and had tried to take his belt and shoes from him in the middle of the restaurant because they were leather and needed to be properly buried to respect the animal that had died for them. It had only taken twenty minutes after he'd finally gotten home (alone) before Lucien had begun to laugh. When he'd related the story to Ben and Léo the next day, he'd laughed so hard that tears had streamed down his face.

But this... this blatant attempt to matchmake between him and Simon was inexcusable. He'd seen Malik and Léo whispering to Ben, surely telling him about Lucien's teenage crush—he was almost certain they didn't know it had lingered into adulthood—and that Simon was reputedly bisexual. Ben, as much as Lucien adored him, was completely unsubtle and lacking in cool, as evidenced by the way he'd all but tied Simon to a chair to convince him to stay. And Malik's little crack about bedrooms was deserving of truly evil vengeance.

On the other hand.... Lucien glanced around the room, at his friends and the man he'd fantasized about for half his life gathered in his home (well, one of them), drinking and laughing and enjoying themselves, and the knot of embarrassment eased. Who cared? Did it matter if Simon guessed that he was attracted to him? Did it matter that his friends had been heavy-handed in trying to make something happen?

No. What mattered was that Lucien was in one of his favorite places with some of his favorite people, he had a lovely weekend ahead of him, and was finally going to be able to give underprivileged kids the opportunity to pursue their dreams through football. He was going to work closely with a man he'd idolized for years, and if this program was successful—and Lucien would make sure it was—then he'd have the leverage to convince his father to back similar programs in dance, art, swimming, and other sports and activities that routinely got overlooked.

Really, life was good.

Malik dropped down heavily beside him on the sofa, and Lucien adjusted his grip on his glass to avoid spilling. The martinis were rather good, if he did say so himself.

"Are you angry?" Malik asked in a low voice— in French. They normally spoke in a mix of English and French around Ben, to facilitate both ease of conversation and Ben's growing ability to speak French, but Simon spoke only English, so Lucien was rather surprised that Malik had switched languages.

"No, not angry," he replied. "I was… not happy, but it really doesn't matter, does it?" He waved a hand dismissively, and Malik grinned.

"Good. We're only acting in your best interests."

Lucien raised a brow. "Really? *Really,* Malik?"

His friend drained his glass and then filched Lucien's and took a drink from it. It was nothing he hadn't done in the past, but Lucien took sudden note of Malik's glassy eyes and realized he'd already had quite a bit to drink—and he'd only arrived a short time ago.

"Is everything all right, Malik?" Malik flinched, and Lucien sat up straight, all thoughts of vengeance gone. "What is it?"

Malik took a deep breath, and Lucien braced himself… and then Malik's trademark winning smile came out, and he knew he would get nothing more out of his friend that night.

"Of course we're acting in your best interests! This is an amazing opportunity for you—how many people get the chance to hook up with their celebrity crushes? And if I understand what you were telling us before, he can't escape you for five years!"

"Can't escape me?" Lucien parried, making a mental note to ask Léo if he knew what was going on with Malik. It was probably more family drama—Malik's father could be a real despot. "That sounds very close to criminal,

Malik. And the next five years are part of the problem. Even if I were inclined to act on my teenage crush, I need to work with the man. This program is important. I can't do anything that would put it at risk."

Malik's smile dimmed a little, and understanding crossed his face. "I know how much you've wanted to start a football scholarship. Okay, we'll stop pushing. But I think you should take a shot anyway. You don't know that you'd be putting anything at risk." He raised his voice and switched to English. "In the meantime, we need to teach Ben about football so he can be useful."

Ben groaned. "Are you high? There's no way my brain will be able to absorb anything sports related."

"You watch football with us sometimes," Malik pointed out.

"No, I watch footballers," Ben retorted. "I couldn't give a crap what's happening with the ball, but I don't mind checking out what's happening in those shorts."

Lucien laughed, his gaze on Simon, who was grinning.

"It's all good for ticket sales," he said, and even Ben laughed at that.

HOURS later, Lucien lay in the dark and wondered what would happen if he were to venture down the hall and slip into Simon's bed. Would he be outraged? Surprised but accepting?

Or welcoming?

Lucien groaned and rolled to his side. Regardless of how such an overture would be received, his arguments to Malik were valid. This program was important. If he and Simon had sex, that could complicate things, and they needed to work together—work *well* together—for five years.

Would it complicate things, though? After all, they were both adults. Both sexually experienced—very, in fact. Weren't they both capable of a one-night stand or even a purely sexual relationship?

Maybe Malik was right and he should take a shot.

Except… would it be a purely sexual relationship? If he were being honest with himself, Lucien had to admit he'd had a crush on Simon Wood for fifteen years, and meeting the man and discovering he was funny, interesting, and socially responsible hadn't exactly killed that crush. Lucien didn't "fall in love" as easily as some others did, but it did seem likely that if his emotions were going to get involved, it would be with a man he'd lusted after for a long time. Plus, Simon had fit in so well with his friends. They'd spent the latter part of the evening in cheerful, semidrunken frivolity, without a single awkward moment once Lucien's friends had given up on the matchmaking.

And while that would be fine if his feelings were returned, if they weren't, it would lead right back to the complicated situation he was so eager to avoid.

Am I overthinking this?

He flipped back onto his back and pulled a pillow over his face. What the hell was wrong with him? Better to stay in his own bed and not tempt disaster. In two days, Simon would be back in England, Lucien would be back in Paris, and he could find someone sweet and uncomplicated to take the edge off his lust without endangering a dream that both he and Simon had apparently both had for a long time.

He and Simon would have to work together for the next five years, but once the program was up and running and secure… well, who knew what the future held?

WHEN Lucien stumbled into his kitchen the next morning, it was to be greeted by the enticing aroma of coffee and the delightful sight of Simon's bare chest. He froze.

"Good morning," Simon said, a little too cheerfully for a man who'd matched Lucien drink for drink the night before. Lucien could hold his liquor—it was a point of pride for him—but even he felt a bit fuzzy the next morning.

"Good morning," he replied. "You're up earlier than I expected." He glanced at the clock on the oven as he made his way toward coffee. It was nearly eight, which was very late for Lucien, even on a weekend, but he knew many others considered it early.

"I can't sleep past seven," Simon said as Lucien fixed himself a cup and then leaned against the counter. Simon was leaning opposite him, the cotton lounge pants the concierge had bought for him slung low on those incredible hips.

Lucien forced his gaze up to meet Simon's hazel one. "Why is that, do you think? A hangover from early morning training?" Had he really asked such a boring question?

Simon shrugged. Lucien had noticed it was a frequent gesture for him. "Nah, it's always been like that, even when I was a little kid. Used to drive Mum crazy on Sunday mornings."

"I can imagine," Lucien said, although he really couldn't. He too had been an early riser as a child, but he didn't think his mother had ever even been aware of that fact. He'd never seen her in the morning until he was bathed and dressed and presented for family breakfast, promptly at seven thirty every weekday and ten on weekends. His parents had always had—and still did have—a rigorous social schedule that meant they often dined out, and so breakfast had been designated as family time.

"What time are we meeting the others for breakfast?" Simon asked. "Oh, and where? Is there a dress code?"

"Nine thirty at the yacht club," Lucien told him. "No jeans, tank tops, or flip-flops, but anything else should be fine."

Simon grinned. "I should be okay, then, since I don't have any of those things with me. I have everything else I need, though—your concierge was incredibly thorough. He even got me shoes and socks."

Lucien nodded. "He's very good at his job. I tried to headhunt him for one of our businesses in Paris, but he refuses to leave the area." Lucien didn't think he needed to mention that the owners' corporation management company that looked after the building was owned by the Morel Corporation, and so the man technically worked for him anyway. The job he'd had in mind had been different.

"Lucky for me this weekend," Simon commented, and went to rinse his cup.

Lucien studied the way the soft pants draped over the curves of his ass, and murmured, "Yes, lucky."

Chapter Five

SI followed Lucien into the bistro at the yacht club. He'd been there once before when he and a teammate had spent a weekend in Monaco, years ago, and met a wealthy German football fan eager to show off his "friendship" with two famous footballers, even if they were British. That had been a long time ago, though, and it looked like the décor had been redone since.

Ben and Léo were already seated at the table the maître d'hotel showed them to, but Malik hadn't arrived yet. Si slid into a seat and smiled at the men.

"Good morning."

"Hi!" Ben chirped, grinning. "How'd you sleep?"

"Well, thanks," Si replied, forcing himself not to look at Lucien. To be honest, he'd hoped his host would make a move, but instead he'd spent the night alone. *Maybe I should make the move tonight?*

He'd think about that later. Not at breakfast in a posh yacht club with Lucien's friends.

Malik yanked back the remaining empty chair and sat. "I'm not late," he announced. Léo looked up from his menu, raised an eyebrow, and said nothing. "I'm not," Malik insisted.

"It's fine, we haven't ordered yet," Ben told him. "And even if we had, we would have ordered for you."

"We wouldn't have needed to order for him," Lucien said smugly. "We could have just told the waiter that he was joining us, and the kitchen would have known exactly what to make him."

Si chuckled. "Do you always order the same thing?" he asked Malik, who scowled, but his eyes were twinkling.

"I just know what I like," he responded. Léo opened his mouth to comment, but the waiter approached at that moment, and he shut it again. Si was rather disappointed; the previous evening Léo had proven to have a quick and incisive wit, and seemed to enjoy teasing his cousin and Lucien.

They ordered quickly—in fact, the waiter began writing on his pad the moment he saw Malik—and soon were discussing the scholarship program again. Lucien had brought some of the financial estimates for Léo to look over, and the two of them bent their heads over the documents, muttering in French.

Si sighed and looked at Ben and Malik. "I really need to learn French," he announced.

Ben nodded sagely. "Good for you. It took me a lot longer to come to that conclusion, but I eventually got sick of Léo telling people to speak in English so I wasn't excluded."

"We got sick of it, too," Malik chimed in. "Fortunately for us all, you were a quick learner."

"You didn't speak French before you met Léo?" Si asked, a little surprised—although not sure why.

"Nope." Ben shook his head. "When I arrived in Monaco just under a year ago, I knew maybe half a dozen French words and some of them were foods. Then I met Léo, and he speaks English, so I was really lazy about learning a new language."

"And you were in denial about staying." Malik smirked at Ben over the rim of his water glass, but Ben ignored him.

"So I didn't really start learning in earnest until late last year. It helps being surrounded by native speakers, though."

"I won't have that advantage," Si admitted. "And when I do speak to French people, it'll be on a professional basis, so probably not the time to try out new words."

Their breakfast was served then, and Lucien put away the financial documents as they all settled in to eat.

"Is everything good?" Si asked him and Léo, and Léo nodded.

"I don't think there will be any problems," he said. "I know you have funding covered, but you may want to consider external fundraising anyway. More money can never hurt a program like this."

"Yes," Si said. "I was thinking about publicity of some sort, but hadn't quite gotten to any details yet."

"Are you planning to begin sponsoring for next season?" Malik asked. "Maybe you can tie the selection process in with the publicity."

"No," Ben said firmly, and they all looked at him in surprise. "Remember that the main qualifications for this program are talent and lack of money. How would you feel if someone put a spotlight on you—and your family—that essentially highlighted your financial situation?"

"Good point," Malik conceded. "But that also makes ongoing promotion of the program difficult. You can't hold it up as a success and have incumbents encourage other families to apply if nobody is willing to admit to being a part of it."

"Some people will," Léo said, putting down his fork and picking up his glass. He raised it toward Si. "They'll just have to be volunteers, which means you'll have to wait until the program is running."

"And that brings us back to the question of publicity prior to next season." Lucien narrowed his eyes, seemingly seeing something nobody else could. "The program covers funding for recipients to attend summer training camps, doesn't it?"

"Of course," Si said, wondering where he was going with this. "Off-season camps are essential for development, and the best ones are bloody expensive. I think it would be too ambitious to plan to get any of our kids into camps for this summer, though, since we haven't even opened for applications yet."

"No...." Lucien appeared to be deep in thought. Léo and Malik exchanged glances.

"He has that look," Malik said.

"Yes," Léo agreed.

"What look?" Ben asked. Si glanced at them, then returned his attention to Lucien's face. That expression of intense concentration was so bloody sexy.

"His diabolical plan look," Malik answered Ben.

"Diabolical plan?" The patent disbelief in Léo's voice dragged Si's gaze away from Lucien.

"Well, what would you call it? Every time he got that look in school, we'd end up doing something we shouldn't, and most times got suspended. And ever since then, whenever he gets that look, it costs us a fortune."

Léo sighed. "It is an expensive look," he conceded.

"I can hear you, you know," Lucien said dryly, now staring at his plate, pushing food around with his fork.

"What the hell are you talking about?" Ben demanded, and Si only just refrained from cheering. What the bloody hell *were* they nattering on about?

Léo took Ben's hand, kissed it, and explained, "That's the look Lucien gets when he's had a brilliant idea. Sometimes even he will agree that it's not a viable idea, but mostly he just decides to put as much money behind it as necessary to make it happen."

"Right now," Malik interjected, waving a hand at Lucien, "he's thinking about the details, calculating how it could all be managed—whatever it is."

Si turned back to Lucien, his breakfast abandoned, heart pounding. Lucien had had a brilliant idea about the program? "What's the idea?" he asked, suddenly desperate to know. Lucien just made a shooing gesture with one hand, the other still moving food in random patterns on his plate.

"He won't talk about it until he's done thinking it through," Léo said, and Si heard the sounds of silverware being picked up and the meal resuming. He stared at Lucien for several long seconds more, then forced his attention to the others and picked up his fork.

"Have you been to Monaco many times?" Ben asked him, and Si latched on to the distraction.

"A few. I've never really played tourist, though, so I probably haven't seen half as much as I should have," he admitted. Most of his visits had been in the company of teammates, either for official purposes, or for partying.

"So many people haven't," Ben agreed. "Léo had never even been to the Musée océanographique until I took him last year, and he's been living here for years."

Si blinked. Wasn't that an aquarium? He looked at Léo, who shrugged and aimed a fond smile in Ben's direction. "I haven't either," Si confessed. "To be honest, I never even thought of it. Usually when we came here, it was for parties."

Ben shrugged. "That makes sense. No offense, but professional athletes are usually better known for partying than for cultural experiences."

Si winced, but couldn't disagree. "I like to think I've grown out of the partying phase of my life now, so maybe I can finally appreciate some of the other parts of Monaco. Like the restaurant tonight. I think I've been before—it's at the Hôtel de Paris, isn't it?"

"Yes," Ben said. "Oh—I didn't think, have you got a suit with you?"

Silence fell over the table, and Si's stomach tensed with anticipation. Why hadn't it occurred to him that he'd need a suit for dinner? He'd even been to the restaurant before, for fuck's sake.

"No. If it weren't for Lucien's concierge, I wouldn't even have clean underwear right now." What the hell was he supposed to do? Politely decline dinner? Buy a suit? A tickle of excitement ran down his spine. He'd *love* a new suit—they were kind of a weakness—but would that seem overeager? Which would they expect of him? He sneaked a peek at Lucien, who was still focused on his plate. He was Lucien's houseguest for the weekend, and Lucien was the kind of host who wouldn't let him sit home alone while he went out. "I suppose I need to buy a suit today." *Hooray!*

"Does this feel like déjà vu to anybody else?" Malik asked. Ben elbowed him.

"Shut up. Although...." He frowned. "There are few similarities, aren't there?"

"Similarities?" Si asked, completely lost.

"The first time I went to Le Louis XV, I didn't realize I'd need a suit until that day," Ben explained.

Si blinked. "That is kind of weird," he commented. "I guess that makes us both unprepared?"

Ben raised his glass in salute. "To being unprepared and scraping through anyway."

"Are you drunk?" Léo asked his boyfriend. "You hate being unprepared."

"Because I never know if I'll scrape through," Ben explained. "And no, I'm not drunk! I don't get drunk anymore."

Si wondered briefly how that could be when he'd seen with his own eyes Ben drinking the night before—and unless he was mistaken, sipping at a mimosa right at that moment. Never mind, he had other things to worry about.

"Can you recommend somewhere to get a suit at short notice?" Somewhere nice, he meant. There was no way he'd buy a suit off the rack, and although Monaco abounded with men's clothing stores, finding somewhere that could tailor at the last minute wasn't always so easy. Si was usually not fussy when it came to clothes, but he had to admit that over the years he'd become attached to custom tailoring for suits.

Fine, the truth was, he was a suit diva. His mother and sisters had taken to calling him Barney, after the suit-obsessed character from *How I Met Your Mother*. They just didn't understand how a good-quality suit could....

Yeah, he just liked them.

"Carrere," Malik said, and Si dropped his fork with a loud clatter. *Carrere?* He'd always wanted a Carrere suit, but Carrere made appointments only by referral and invitation, and Si had never known a Carrere client well enough to ask for an introduction. Could this be his chance?

"I didn't know Carrere would do last-minute tailoring," he said, trying to be casual as he picked up his fork, but he was pretty sure his face was red.

"He will if you go with Lucien. He loves Lucien."

"Who loves me?" Lucien asked, and all heads turned toward him.

"Carrere," Léo told him. "You're back with us, are you?"

"I am. Why are we talking about Carrere?"

"Simon needs a suit for dinner tonight," Ben announced. Lucien paused with his glass partway to his mouth.

"I hadn't thought of that," he confessed. "We will go to Carrere directly after breakfast. My apologies, Simon."

His cheeks were definitely red now—either that, or he had a sudden-onset fever. Had Lucien just apologized because Simon didn't have a suit, and basically offered to fix it by taking him to the maestro of suits? Si was pretty sure his romance-novel-loving youngest sister would call that "swoonworthy."

"It's not your fault," he mumbled, then cleared his throat. "Er—so, what brilliant but supposedly expensive idea have you had?"

"And how much is it going to cost me?" Malik chipped in.

Lucien waved one hand while forking food into his mouth with the other. They waited, watching him, while he chewed and swallowed, and Si bit back the urge to laugh hysterically.

"Summer training camp," Lucien finally said.

Si looked at Léo and Malik to see if maybe that was some sort of code. They looked just as blank as he felt.

"Yes, we talked about summer camps," Si replied, trying to be patient. Maybe Lucien had drunk more than he'd realized last night and was a little hungover? "But since we don't actually have anyone in the program yet, and as it's already May, it's unlikely we could get placements in time."

Lucien shook his head. "No, I mean we should run our own camp. Not a full one, of course, but perhaps a week or two toward the end of the summer, when most of the other camps have wound up. It will allow us to build publicity for and launch the program, put all the participants in touch with each other, and raise additional funds by charging a fee for other young players to attend."

Si sat back in his chair, processing. It wasn't a bad idea. "What's the incentive for fee-paying players to attend?" he asked. That was the only catch he could see right off.

Lucien, Malik, and Léo looked at him like he was a moron. "You are," Malik said, his tone implying that perhaps Si needed help tying his own shoes. He blinked.

"Oh." He did feel stupid now. He'd often made appearances and run short programs at youth training camps. Current and former professional players as coaches were one of the biggest attractions for the camps.

"Well, you and whoever of your footballer friends are willing to volunteer," Lucien added. "I don't think you could manage it alone."

Shuddering at the mere thought, Si considered who he could ask. If the camp was going to be at the end of summer, it couldn't be anyone still playing, although they might be able to make an appearance—maybe at the launch Lucien had spoken of. That still left quite a few people he could approach, though, including a former World Cup coach.

"I'll put together a list," he said, "and make some calls, see who would possibly be interested. Would we need permits and licenses? And where would we have it? Which country, I mean."

"Paul will help with those details," Lucien told him. "I'll put it on his list for Monday morning. I think, given the time frame, we will need to pick the location based on how easy it would be to get the relevant permits."

"Yes. And this also means you need to get the program up and running. You'll want to begin publicity for the camp as soon as you can so as to get enrollments, but as soon as the camp is publicized, the program will be in the spotlight, and must be open for applications." Léo frowned slightly. "As soon as you register and license, I can get the accounts set up."

Lucien had pulled out his phone and appeared to be making notes. "Paul can do that on Monday, also," he said, then stopped and looked at Si. "Unless you want to do it, Simon?"

Si drew a deep breath. Did he want to register the program as a charitable body and ensure they were licensed to operate?

Hell yes.

He hadn't realized it would matter, but it did. He wanted to be the one to fill out the forms and submit them, to take that next step to seeing this dream realized.

And somehow, Lucien knew that.

"I'll do it." His voice was a little husky. He cleared his throat. "But we need a name first." That was one of the few details they hadn't settled yet.

"What are the options?" Malik asked, and Si, who'd gone over the list so many times that he'd memorized it, rattled off the prospective names.

The silence that followed said it all. They were good, but none was perfect.

"What are you trying to say?" Ben asked. "The name has to be memorable, but it also needs to encapsulate your purpose. You're working toward the future of soccer."

"Football," Si corrected absently, considering his words. Ben huffed and rolled his eyes.

"Whatever. The thing is, you're empowering kids with talent to build a career, right? Giving them a chance at a future in sports that they might not otherwise be able to achieve. But while it all centers around socc—*football*, it's also still a charity, and you want to attract people with money who know next to nothing about the sport."

"Right," Si said slowly, wondering where he was going with this.

"Don't keep us in suspense, Ben," Lucien urged. Ben flushed but continued.

"So most of the names you're thinking of, those are sports terms, aren't they? I mean, I'm guessing, because I didn't recognize any of them."

"They are," Léo told him, and Ben nodded.

"Okay, so that's good for everyone who loves s—football, but your cashed-up prospective donors might not all be fans. They might just be people looking for a tax break, and so the name has to catch their attention and give them some idea of what the charity does. 'Give and Go' is catchy, whatever it means, but it sounds like a drive-through charity. As a non-sports lover, I don't immediately connect it to sport."

Léo leaned over and kissed his boyfriend. "Sometimes I forget how amazing you are," he murmured. "And then you remind me."

A pang of longing took Si by surprise. *Well, that's new.* He'd never particularly wished for a relationship or a happy ever after, always assuming it would happen when and if it was going to, but it seemed retirement was awakening new desires in him.

"Ben, you're exactly right," he said, pushing aside the sudden longing for a partner to lean on and have tell him that he was amazing.

"Yes," Lucien added, looking chagrined. "We were so taken by the idea of a catchy football term that we overlooked the purpose of the name."

Ben's cheeks were flaming, but he grinned. "Well, it's nice to know I can be useful sometimes. Now… names. You need a keyword that immediately brings *football* to mind, or at least sports. Play?"

"Ball," Malik said decisively. "There are enough sports that use a ball that the word is almost synonymous with sport."

"Ball, ball, ball…." Si chanted, trying to think of something catchy.

"Balls, balls, balls," Malik murmured, a leering inflection to his tone that made them all laugh.

"You don't even like balls that way," Ben accused, throwing his napkin at Malik, who shrugged.

"It just came to me." He winked.

"You're not helping," Lucien told him. "Concentrate."

"Have a ball?" Malik offered, a wicked glint in his eye suggesting he was still not being entirely serious.

"I like that it suggests fun, but no," Si said.

Léo snapped his fingers. "On the Ball."

Click.

Si and Lucien looked at each other, and Lucien raised a brow. "It's your baby," he said, and Si grinned.

"On the Ball it is."

Chapter Six

LUCIEN led Simon away from Carrere's establishment and back toward his car. Well, it was closer to *dragged* than *led*. Who would have guessed that the usually casual ex-footballer would be so enamored of suits?

Simon was still chattering about fabric and cut, and Lucien smirked. In addition to begging for a quickly altered sample to wear to dinner, which they'd need to return for in a few hours, Simon had also ordered three new suits with shirts to match.

"Where are we going?" Simon asked, interrupting his own monologue on the benefits of couture tailoring as they walked past the garage where Lucien had parked the car.

"For a walk," Lucien said vaguely. In actual fact, he wasn't sure—passing the car had been an accident, but he wasn't willing to admit that. It didn't really matter where they went, as long as he got Simon away from the salon. As fond as he himself was of a well-tailored suit, he didn't feel the need to spend all of a beautiful Saturday in Monaco weighing the merits of different suit linings. "To clear our heads," he added.

Simon shrugged. "Right-oh," he said, shoving his hands in his pockets. They strolled along for a few moments, Lucien wracking his brain for a possible destination. Monaco was only a few kilometers from end to end, and it wouldn't be long until they were walking in France. Back to his apartment or the club? Or something else?

"I was thinking," Simon began, and Lucien turned to him in relief. "We're planning to promote the program through club teams, but what about kids who don't even think about clubs because of the expense? They won't have any contacts there who could tell them about scholarships."

"So we need a wider profile, outside the football circle," Lucien said slowly. "Schools? They don't focus a lot on any one sport in physical education classes, but teachers should be able to spot anybody with outstanding ability. Or at the least, maybe there would be a notice board in the gym where a flyer for the program could be pinned."

Simon nodded enthusiastically. "Yeah. And community centers. They always have notice boards, and since they usually offer free or low-cost facilities and activities, people hang out there."

"A literature campaign," Lucien said decisively. "It's too late now to contact the schools this academic year, since we won't have anything for them before they close for the summer, but community centers will definitely see more kids soon, and we can be ready for the schools in September." He pulled out his phone and noted the idea, then began adding details of what should be included in the information packets to schools and the flyers.

"Hey!" Simon jerked him back, his grip on Lucien's arm painful. Horns blared, and Lucien blinked and looked up.

He'd just been saved from stepping out onto an extremely busy road. He jumped back.

"I'm sorry, Simon," he apologized, stepping back farther from the road. "I am not normally so inattentive." Never had he been so unaware of his surroundings.

"Yeah, well, maybe be more careful, okay?" Simon's face was white, and his gaze kept jumping to the cars whizzing past. "I don't want anything to happen to you."

The words hung between them, and Lucien's heartbeat sped up. He swallowed. Could Simon mean that maybe he was... fond of Lucien? They'd only known each other a day, but being together continuously, with the addition of—dare he hope—lust, could easily lead to personal feelings.

Should he say something?

What should he say?

Simon stepped back and chuckled, and the spell was broken. "I need you to get this program running," he said, and Lucien forced himself to chuckle also. They turned and walked back the way they had come.

"Let's get the car," Lucien said. He was unaccustomed to walking for transportation purposes, and found it an inefficient use of time. It took too long, and the time couldn't even be spent multitasking.

LATE that evening, they strolled out of the Hôtel de Paris after a lovely—as usual—meal at Le Louis XV. The night was warm, and with the impending Grand Prix, the number of tourists wandering around had increased.

"What would we like to do?" Malik asked. "It's a lovely evening, and still early."

"We could get ice cream?" Ben said, looking across the square at the Café de Paris.

Simon made a small sound of protest.

"You just had dessert," Léo chided fondly. "How can you want ice cream right now?"

"I always want ice cream," Ben answered with a cheeky wink.

Lucien groaned. "Please, don't start being all cute now," he begged. Léo had some sort of weird obsession with Ben eating ice cream, and Lucien was already sexually frustrated. He didn't need to watch two of his best friends flirting.

"The casino?" Simon suggested, looking over at the lit building. Lucien felt a stab of disappointment.

"Nah," Ben said before Lucien could speak. "Lucien doesn't like the casino unless they have a tournament or something on that's interesting to watch."

Lucien felt Simon's gaze on him, and forced himself to meet it. "You don't like to gamble?" Simon asked.

He shook his head. "But I have no objection to others doing so." He didn't want Simon to think he was being judgmental. It was simply that straight-up cash gambling bored him. After all, the outcome was completely irrelevant to him—win or lose, it didn't matter. It was just money.

A bright flash had them all turning to the left. Several young men were huddled together about ten feet away, pointing phones in their direction and muttering to each other.

"I think Simon's been recognized," Malik said quietly. Lucien shot Simon a look. He had a fixed smile on his face and had turned so his back was to the men, but Lucien knew that wouldn't work for long. Either the group would work up the courage to come and speak to him, or someone else would notice him. Or both.

"Let's go," Léo said. "Back to your place, Lucien. The security is good, and Simon won't have to leave again tonight."

Simon groaned as they started walking toward the valets. "I'm sorry," he muttered. "It's gotten better since I retired."

"Not your fault," Léo murmured as the valets saw them coming and scurried to fetch their cars. Lucien glanced over his shoulder and noticed that the young men had been joined by more people, and that there was some pointing and gesturing going on.

"Whichever car comes first, Simon gets in," he murmured, just loud enough for his friends to hear. They agreed, Malik also eyeing the crowd. He muttered under his breath.

"Simon, if they come over, what do you want to do?" Malik asked, somewhat urgently, and Lucien glanced over his shoulder again. Had the crowd moved closer, or did it just look that way because it had grown? There were nearly two dozen people looking their way now, phones out and flashing, and Lucien was pretty sure it wouldn't be long before distant photos wouldn't be enough for them.

Simon sighed. "Sign autographs and have some quick photos," he said grimly. "Now is not the time to court negative publicity," he added, and Lucien winced. They'd spent most of the day talking about how to attract publicity for On the Ball, and having some whiny twentysomething's tweet about Simon Wood snubbing fans go viral would not help their cause.

Why was it taking the valets so long? Lucien looked around, and noticed more people beginning to cluster throughout the Place du Casino, all looking toward them, some excited, some curious. Most were blocking the road, though.

"Malik, I see your car right behind those tourists," he said, nodding in that direction. "Let's walk that way. If anyone stops us, Simon can sign, but we keep moving toward the car."

"Good idea," Léo said, placing his arm around Ben. He leaned over and murmured to the valet supervisor, who nodded and said something back. Léo flashed a grin. "The casino will send out security if things get out of control," he told them as they started walking casually toward Malik's McLaren. "They want to avoid it if possible because technically they have no power outside the casino, but if necessary someone will come to keep the crowd back."

Lucien sent up silent thanks that Léo and Ben were so fond of the Salle Blanche, and thus so well-known by the casino staff. They were closer to the car now, close enough to see the frustration on the face of the valet driving it, and Lucien held out hope that maybe they'd get Simon in and away before the crowd realized what they were doing.

His car appeared, slowly inching through the tourists, and he spotted Léo's behind it. *How are we going to leave without running anyone over?* he wondered, then decided it was better to worry about that once it was actually an issue.

"Simon!"

Damn. Too late. He eyed the distance to the car even as Simon turned toward the young man who'd shouted and was now jogging toward them. He grabbed Simon's arm and tugged. "Keep moving," he murmured. "He can come to you. Remember, we have no crowd control." He'd seen how out of control situations like this could become, and he wasn't going to stand by and watch Simon be assaulted or trampled by enthusiastic fans.

They gained a few more feet toward the car, were actually level with the front bumper, when the boy caught up to them.

"Simon, hi! Can I get a selfie with you?" he asked in French, grinning broadly, his face lit up with excitement, and Lucien felt a pang of guilt. This boy was so genuinely thrilled to meet an idol, and all Lucien could think about was getting away.

"Simon doesn't speak French," Ben said gently, while Léo translated for Simon, and Malik walked around the car and waited for the valet to get out.

"Tell him a selfie is fine, but just one," Simon said, smiling kindly at his fan. Ben quickly translated, and the moment the boy stepped up next to Simon and lifted his phone, the dam broke. Shouts erupted, and the sound of running feet echoed through the Place du Casino.

"Let's go," Léo said grimly, yanking open the passenger door of the McLaren. Malik was already behind the wheel. Lucien took Simon's arm again and pulled him away from the swelling crowd. Phone cameras were flashing from all directions, and people were shouting in multiple languages, begging Simon for photos, autographs, asking if he wanted to get a drink, if he was in Monaco for the Grand Prix, what he planned to do with his retirement... and several offers for "company" that evening. Lucien raised a brow at one *very* interesting suggestion, and wondered how Simon would have felt about it if he'd understood German.

Using his elbows, he pushed through the crowd, Simon pressed up close to him. It was only a few feet to the door Léo was guarding, but it felt like miles. Where had all these people come from? Something flew over the crowd and landed on the open door of the car, and Lucien flinched back, half turning to shield Simon, fearing the worst. *Wait, is that...?*

Someone had thrown underwear. White silky panties with little pink roses on them. Not sure whether to laugh or curse—were they an invitation, or a sign of derision?—Lucien pressed forward, finally reaching his destination. Léo moved aside and they ushered Simon into the passenger seat, Léo taking a moment to brush the panties off the door with his arm before he carefully slammed it closed.

The tinted windows provided some measure of protection, but with the crowd pressing in, the car was unable to go anywhere. One determined fan actually threw herself onto the bonnet, and Lucien winced. Malik would not be happy.

In fact, it must have spurred Malik to act, because the car inched forward, slowly, but definitely moving. The crowd was left with no option but to move, although they pressed against the sides of the car.

"This is ridiculous," Ben said from beside Lucien, and he glanced at his friend, wondering where he'd been. "Seriously, what do they think they're going to gain from this?" The disgust in his voice was clear. "The police will be here soon."

"Will they?" Lucien asked.

Ben held up his phone. "They said they would."

Léo leaned over and kissed his boyfriend. "At least one of us was thinking," he said. "We should have gone into the casino or back into the hotel, and called the police to control the crowd."

"Hindsight," Lucien murmured, watching the slow progress of Malik's car. He was just coming to the front of the casino and still had to circle around the other side of the Place du Casino before he would make it to a more open road.

Fortunately that was when the police arrived.

As officers began clearing the crowd from the car and forcing people back, many lost interest and wandered off. Lucien, Léo, and Ben stood and watched until Malik was able to accelerate smoothly out of the Place du Casino, even as people still tried to take photos of the car.

"We'd better go," Léo said. "They're not going to be able to get into the building without you."

Lucien blinked, then mentally kicked himself. "I was so caught up in getting them away from here, I didn't think the rest through," he confessed as they walked toward their cars, now idling in front of the casino.

"I think we were all in that boat," Ben said dryly.

Lucien was just getting into his car when his phone rang. He glanced at the screen as he bucked his seat belt. Malik.

"Are you both okay?" he asked, not bothering with a greeting.

"Yes," Malik answered. "Although I for one am eternally thankful that my money came via inheritance, and not fame."

"I agree," Lucien said, pulling away from the casino.

"Are you on your way? We're nearly at your building, and while I can park in a guest spot, the concierge won't let us up if you're not there."

"I know. I'm coming now—three minutes," he promised. He disconnected the call and concentrated on not hitting pedestrians as he zoomed through the streets. Several minutes later, he pulled into the parking garage under his building, noted Malik's McLaren in one of the guest spots, and hit the remote button on his visor to open the gate into the residents' parking area.

By the time he'd parked his car, Malik and Simon had gotten out of the car and come through to wait at the residents' elevator. The one that serviced guest parking only went as far as the lobby, where the concierge would ensure guests were invited before letting them go farther. Léo was just parking as Lucien got out of his car, and he waited near the gate, preventing it from closing until Léo and Ben could join him. Together they walked to the elevator, where Malik had jabbed the call button.

"Are you okay?" Lucien asked Simon, who flushed.

"Yes, thank you," he replied. "I'm so sorry."

"Not your fault," Ben said cheerfully. "Although, hell! I don't envy you having to go through that. Is it always so intense?"

The elevator doors opened, and they walked in.

"No," Simon said ruefully. "At official publicity events there's security to keep everything under control, and mostly when I'm on my own, I don't just stand around. I think they just had too much time to think about it. I'm out of practice dealing with fans."

"It's fine," Lucien assured him. "And I'm sure Ben is already practicing how he will tell Dani."

"Hey!" Ben protested as the elevator stopped at Lucien's floor and the doors opened.

"Aren't you?" Léo asked as they shuffled into the hallway and Lucien dug out his key. Ben declined to respond, his face mutinous.

"Who's Dani?" Simon asked. Lucien opened the door and stood back to let everyone in.

"His best friend in Australia," Malik answered. "They talk all the time." As if on cue, Ben's phone trilled. Lucien knew it was Ben's because of the immensely annoying ringtone.

He gestured for everyone to go into the living room, and closed the front door. When he joined his guests, Ben had his phone to his ear and had his hand extended to Léo, who was pulling his phone from his pocket.

"What do you mean, I'm accidentally all over the internet?" Ben was demanding. He snatched Léo's phone and began tapping at the screen, wedging his own phone between his ear and his shoulder.

"He knows those phones have a speaker function, right?" Simon asked Lucien quietly.

Lucien smiled. "Probably, but he gets distracted."

"*Oh my God!*" Ben yelled.

Simon sighed. "I'm so sorry."

Annoyance surged in Lucien. It was not right that going out to dinner with friends meant Simon had to apologize for their privacy being invaded. "Stop saying that," he said. "You owe us no apology."

"Look at this," Ben demanded, turning Léo's phone toward them. "Some moron has started a thread on Twitter claiming that Simon, Lucien, and Malik are in a three-way!"

Lucien blinked. *A three-way what?* His English vocabulary caught up a moment later, by which time Malik had snatched the phone from Ben and begun to read the tweets aloud, but was laughing so hard his words were mostly unintelligible.

Léo grabbed the phone. "Use your own," he said when Malik protested. Ben leaned against his lover and craned his neck to see the phone screen, while telling Dani, "Yes, I'm reading it now... no, I haven't seen Facebook or Instagram. How have these people had time to do all this? It happened like five minutes ago!"

Tuning them out for the time being, Lucien turned to Simon, who was looking at his own phone. "Are you okay?" he asked quietly, feeling like he'd asked that question entirely too many times this evening.

Simon looked up and smiled, but it was strained. "This is not the kind of publicity we wanted," he said, and the expression in his eyes was worried.

"Of course it is," Malik said, dropping into Lucien's most comfortable armchair, the one he'd had made for each of his homes because he loved it so much. "It's easily dismissible as silly gossip, and puts you squarely in the limelight for the announcement of On the Ball."

"That's true," Lucien agreed, eager to banish Simon's anxiety. "Sit down and relax. Would you like a drink?"

"I think that's a good idea," Léo said. "Let's have a drink." He put his arm around Ben and steered him to one of the sofas, and Lucien touched Simon's arm and smiled encouragingly.

"Sit," he said again, and went to find the excellent bottle of cognac he'd bought a few years back.

Several minutes later, they were all settled in, drinks in hand. Malik and Ben were still glued to their phones.

"Somebody needs to explain this to me," Lucien said, leaning back on the sofa and trying to convince himself that he'd sat so close to Simon by accident. "Why am I having a three-way with Malik and Simon?"

"Because we're both incredibly attractive and sexy?" Malik asked. Lucien snorted.

"That may be, but I think you're too much man for me," he replied dryly. Simon choked on his cognac, and for a moment Lucien feared he'd offended him, but a moment later that fear was allayed when Simon burst out laughing.

Warmth spread through his chest, and Lucien smiled softly, glad he'd been able to lighten Simon's mood. He watched the ex-footballer settle back in his seat, grinning.

"Someone tweeted photos," Ben said. "One of you holding Simon's arm and pulling him away from the crowd, and another of Simon in Malik's car. Someone else tweeted a reply that I think was probably meant to be a joke, something about Simon being with two guys in one night, and then someone who recognized you and Malik tweeted that you were friends, and... it just seems to have snowballed from there." His phone dinged, and he looked down at it. "Dani," he said, swiping the screen. "She says we should avoid checking news headlines."

Simon groaned and reached for his phone, which was on the coffee table. Lucien caught his hand. "Don't," he said, but before he could continue, his own phone rang— with his father's ringtone. He stiffened. *News headlines.* "I need to take this," he said, pulling it from his pocket. "Don't look." He stood and answered the phone as he left the room and headed toward his bedroom, unaccountably nervous. While sensational press had been a common feature of their youth, it had been a long time since any of them had featured in the media spotlight for the wrong reasons. "Good evening, Father."

"Lucien, *what* are you doing?" Édouard sounded exasperated but also slightly amused, which was a great relief to Lucien. Chiding phone calls had once been a regular element of his relationship with his father, but not one he was keen to go back to.

"Not what you think," he said lightly. "Léo, Ben, Malik, Simon, and I had dinner at Le Louis XV, and we were waiting for our cars when some tourists recognized Simon. It got out of hand."

"I wasn't aware that you were friends with Simon Wood," his father said, and Lucien realized that he'd mentioned Simon's name as casually as if they'd been friends for years.

"We met yesterday to discuss plans for the football scholarship program." *Was that only yesterday?* "I had to leave London, but we weren't finished, so Simon came with me. We worked on the program most of last evening and today." He hesitated. "He is a friend now, I think."

"I see." It was all Édouard said, but Lucien was suddenly uncomfortably aware that his father knew exactly who his idol had been when he was a teenager.

"I haven't seen the headlines yet. Are they terrible?" he asked, in an attempt to redirect the conversation at least slightly.

His father huffed, and it was a sound Lucien had heard so many times before that he found it comforting. "They are not terrible," he conceded. "Mostly it is just a quick mention that Simon was seen this evening in Monaco, that police were called for crowd control, and that he was in your company—and Malik's and Léo's. There was a reference to online speculation, and that was what our public relations director called me about."

Lucien winced. "I am aware of the online speculation," he said, just as a crash from the living room caused him to jerk his head around. What was going on?

"Good. At this stage, we are taking no action," Édouard told him. "This is foolish, groundless gossip, and we are ignoring it as beneath our notice. However, it may be best if you announce your new project sooner rather than later. Are plans progressing?"

"Yes," Lucien assured him forcing himself to concentrate on the conversation, "and our intention was to register the charity on Monday. As soon as that's done, we will arrange the press release."

"Excellent," his father approved. "Don't worry, Lucien. You may have had a wild childhood, but your behavior as an adult has always been above reproach. Your reputation can withstand some foolish rumors that nobody with sense would believe."

"Thank you." He wondered when he'd become so boring that he was considered "above reproach." "I will keep you informed." They said goodbye, and Lucien returned to his friends. He paused in the doorway, noting what appeared to be the shattered remains of an iPhone. Léo had his phone to his ear while Malik glared at the pieces of his, Ben's arm wrapped around his shoulders and Simon handing him another drink. Lucien cringed as he realized that if his father had seen the headlines, so too would have Léo's and Malik's.

"I'm so—"

"Don't say you're sorry," Malik interrupted Simon as Lucien joined them. Malik met his inquiring gaze. "The usual bullshit," he informed him. "If he hadn't used this as an excuse to call, he would have found another one." He knocked back his drink, and Lucien just nodded, familiar enough with the dynamic of Malik's relationship with his father to know not to ask questions.

Lucien raised an eyebrow in Léo's direction. "Charles is taking this worse than I expected," he commented, surprised Léo was still on the phone. Ben snorted.

"No, Charles called, told Léo to try to avoid such crass publicity, and then hung up. He's talking to Miryam now."

Lucien winced. At least he hadn't been subjected to a call from his mother. He went to get them another round of drinks.

"I don't know what she's so upset about. Léo was barely mentioned at all," Malik said, scowling at his cousin. Léo, wrapping up the call, glared right back. A moment later he tossed his phone on the coffee table.

"She's upset about *you*. Apparently, she's failed you as an aunt, and her sister as guardian to you while you live away from home."

Bending his head as he carefully poured, Lucien tried his best to hide his grin. It was unnecessary, however, as Malik was already laughing.

Chapter Seven

SI rolled over in bed. It was somewhere in the wee hours, because he hadn't gotten to bed until after one and he felt refreshed enough that he must have slept for several hours at least, but no light was peeking around the curtains.

He lay there, staring into the darkness. In less than forty-eight hours, it felt like his life had turned completely upside down. Not quite two days ago he'd been lying awake in his own bed, unable to sleep because he'd been nervous about his meeting with Lucien Morel. It seemed like a lifetime ago.

Sighing, he threw back the sheet and sat up, reaching over to flip on the bedside lamp. Now that he was awake, he had to go to the bathroom, and he was kind of thirsty.

He took care of business and then quietly made his way to the kitchen. The light over the stove was on, and he frowned at it. He was sure all the lights had been off in here when he and Lucien had gone to bed.

"You could not sleep?"

Si jumped, his heart somersaulting into his throat, and gasped as he spun. Lucien was leaning in the doorway. "Christ on a crutch, mate, you scared the hell out of me!" He put a hand on his chest and took a deep breath, willing his heartbeat back to normal. "How the bloody hell do you move so quietly?"

Lucien grinned. "Apologies. I didn't mean to startle you."

Shaking his head, Si let his hand drop and smiled back. "No harm done, I suppose. I was thirsty. What has you up?" He turned back to the cabinet where the glassware was, and got himself a glass. As he filled it with water, he heard Lucien coming into the kitchen and crossing the room. He looked up to see the blond man leaning on the bench near the sink.

He wasn't wearing a shirt.

How did I not notice that before? Oh, right, I was trying to keep from pissing myself in fright. I'm noticing now, though. Wow.

For a businessman, Lucien was built awfully nicely. Si wondered if all those people who had meetings with him knew that the Morel heir had a six-pack under his perfectly tailored suits and just enough golden hair on his chest to enhance his bitable pecs.

"I could not sleep, so I thought I would do some work. But I could not concentrate on that, either."

Si drank his water, letting the velvet tones of Lucien's voice and that delicious accent wash over him.

"Something bothering you?" he asked, putting his glass in the sink, then deciding maybe he should wash it. Anything to keep his hands busy so they wouldn't defy his brain and reach for Lucien.

Professional, Si. You have to work with this man for the next five years. Besides, you're still not entirely sure he's even interested in men.

Some of the comments made that day would indicate yes, Lucien was attracted to men, but Si knew better than to make assumptions.

Lucien sighed. "No. Yes. No, nothing is bothering me."

Drying the glass, Si remained silent for a long moment, giving Lucien the opportunity to change his mind and share if he wanted to. By the time he'd put the glass away and hung up the tea towel, Lucien still hadn't said anything.

Time for a change of subject.

"Will Malik be okay? He seemed fine when he left, but this isn't likely to cause trouble for him, is it?"

Tension Si hadn't even noticed eased out of Lucien's shoulders, and he straightened from his slouch against the bench. "He will be fine. He and his father are constantly at odds, and this was something new to argue over."

Si wasn't sure that that was exactly reassuring, but if nobody else was worried about it, he wouldn't be, either. "And your father? How did he react?" He hadn't got the chance to ask that earlier, and it was likely part of the reason he'd been unable to sleep.

Lucien shrugged and took a step closer. "He was annoyed that it happened, but of the opinion that it is just foolishness and will blow over. He would, however, like us to announce the program as soon as we can, so we must be… what is that expression about ships?"

"Ships?" Si asked, bewildered. The program was for football, not sailing—right?

"Yes." Lucien looked both frustrated and amused. "When all the people are needed to complete a task."

Si blinked and then realization hit like a bolt of lightning. "Oh! Do you mean, all hands on deck?"

"That is the one. We must be all hands on deck to get things in process."

Smiling a little foolishly—who knew a language barrier could make someone so adorable?—Si nodded. "Absolutely. First thing Monday morning, I'll start the registration process. I imagine word will get out then, even if we don't make any official announcements." Lucien stepped closer still, and the breath caught in Si's throat. There was barely two feet between them now, and the dimness of the room closed around them, intimate. The low light turned Lucien's skin a warm golden color, reflected off his hair.

Si swallowed hard, aware that the soft cotton sleep pants he was wearing did nothing to hide his erection.

"Do you know," Lucien began conversationally, but his voice was rough, "when I was a teenager, you were my idol?"

The words were like a bucket of cold water to Si. He'd given up fucking football groupies a long time ago. Drawing in a deep breath, he stepped back—and was stopped when Lucien stepped forward and caught hold of his arm.

"You were always so honest and upfront with the media," Lucien continued. "You seemed so sure of who you were and what you wanted."

Si stilled. That sounded like genuine appreciation for him as a person, and not just his football talent and fame. *Dangerous territory, Si.*

"But it was the rumors that really got me. You see, I was so confused. Around me, all my friends were infatuated with breasts, with soft female bodies. And I was too—but I also obsessed over pecs, over broad shoulders and five o'clock shadows. I didn't understand—was there something wrong with me? Then I heard the rumors that you were bisexual. I didn't know what that meant, so I looked it up... and I knew I was normal."

He's bi. Si could feel his pulse throbbing at the base of his throat in time with a different throbbing much lower down. *He's bi, and I think he's coming on to me.* Lucien reached out and laid his hand on Si's shoulder, big and warm, and then let it slide down to the middle of his chest. *He's definitely coming on to me.*

What do I do?

I know what I want... but I need to be professional. Fuck it.

Si lunged forward and pressed his lips to Lucien's, sending him stumbling back a step before he recovered and clutched Si to him.

"So the rumor was true?" Lucien gasped between kisses.

"Yep. So bloody true," Si muttered, glorying in the taste of those lips and the feel of all that velvety skin and muscle under his hands.

"Good."

They stopped speaking then, the silence of the apartment broken only by gasps and soft groans as they let hands and mouths explore. Si couldn't get enough of Lucien's body, the soft skin and coarse hair over hard planes, and all of it so warm. And his taste...

had anything in the history of flavor ever tasted so good? Every touch, every movement seemed to send electricity buzzing through him. He'd felt attraction before, had great—even brilliant—sex before, but he'd never felt this vibe in his life, this energy that just touching Lucien sent coursing throughout his body.

Could it get better?

He slid a hand down over that lovely six-pack, lingering only slightly, and brushed his fingers along the line of Lucien's sleep pants. Lucien moaned, broke their kiss, and stripped naked right there in the kitchen. The sight of all that toned, golden, aroused flesh ramped Si's erection from enthusiastic to painful, and in seconds he was naked too. Then they were tangled together again, mouths locked in the hottest damn kiss he'd ever had while their hands pumped each other's dicks.

It was… it was… fuck, there was no word to describe how it felt. Or if there was, his brain wasn't functioning well enough to think of it.

Right.

That was the word. It was *right*. Arousing, yes. Electric, yes. Satisfying—well, it was certainly headed in that direction. But more than anything else, it just felt right. He was meant to be here, doing this, touching Lucien, being touched by Lucien, their mouths and bodies melded together. Lucien was meant to be here with him.

Dangerous.

When Si pulled away for air, he gasped, "I'm not going to last much longer."

Lucien's blue gaze met his, almost electric in its intensity. "Come. Come on me."

That did it for Si. Orgasm took over all his faculties as he came harder than he could ever remember doing in his life. He was vaguely aware that Lucien was coming too, that hot seed was spraying over his chest and stomach, but all that mattered was Lucien's grip on his cock as he milked him dry.

When Si finally caught his breath, he straightened and took a step back. "That was…."

"Incredible?" Lucien supplied, and they smiled at each other.

"Yeah."

Lucien went to the sink, opened the cabinet beneath it, and took out a roll of paper towels. He ripped some off, dampened them, and in short order had them both cleaned up and dressed. Si just stood, bemused and kind of turned on by his efficiency.

Who knew I'd be so attracted to a capable business type? he wondered. Then again, power was attractive, and Lucien had it in spades. *Not to mention he's hot— and blond. You've always had a thing for blonds.*

And nice. He was nice too. Cared about his friends. Funny. Loved football and gave a crap about others.

Oh, bollocks. You're falling for him. After two days? What the fuck is wrong with you? When did you become a Harlequin heroine?

Si shook the thought out of his head. He was *not* falling for Lucien. Just because he appreciated that he was a genuinely good guy, would make an amazing friend, *and* was hot, didn't mean he was getting emotionally involved. He couldn't. That would make things incredibly messy.

Fuck.

He looked up to find Lucien staring at him, a tiny, amused smile on those well-shaped, really soft lips that would be brilliant around his—

Stop.

"You're thinking very hard," Lucien said, and Si pulled himself together.

"Yeah. Um, just thinking about the program." Internally, he winced as Lucien raised a brow. "I mean, this is something I've wanted for a really long time, and I wouldn't want things to be awkward between us." *Like they are right now.*

To his relief, Lucien was still smiling. "Because we must be able to work well together for the next five years," he said, and Si nodded, thrilled that he hadn't been misunderstood. "We are both grown men, both experienced. I believe we can agree that what we do away from the program can remain separate."

Si kept nodding, beginning to feel like a bobble-head doll. "Yes. And... discreet? I don't want people to think the funding—"

"Of course."

They stood there, seemingly in complete agreement, and yet the moment was still awkward. Until Lucien raised a brow and said, "My bed is very comfortable."

Well hell, that was an invitation if ever Si had heard one, and not one he was about to turn down. With a grin, he headed out of the kitchen and down the corridor toward the bedrooms, Lucien following.

Life couldn't be better. He had the charitable program he'd been working toward for twenty years, *and* a hot blond to warm his bed in a no-strings discreet affair.

He ignored the hollow feeling in his chest.

SI leaned back in his desk chair with a real sense of satisfaction. In the nearly six weeks since his return from Monaco, On the Ball had gone from a concept on paper to reality. They were now fully registered and licensed to operate as a charity within the EU—the process sped up to light speed somehow by the Morel Corporation's contacts, thanks to Lucien's indispensable assistant, Paul. They'd also contracted with a graphic design and marketing company to begin design of their promotional materials and website. That had been a lucky stroke—the award-winning boutique company had agreed to do the work for free in return for being named as one of On the Ball's key sponsors. The owner had privately confided to Si that it was great exposure to be so closely associated with the Morel Corporation. Si had made a mental note, hoping to use that to get other discounted and free services. They had a healthy budget allocation for all the services they would require, but every cent they saved in those areas was another cent toward sponsoring kids.

Rumors were already circulating, and he'd been contacted by several sports journalists to confirm. So far, he'd been able to hold them off, pending an official announcement of On the Ball's purpose, but as soon as the website was ready to go and people who were interested had somewhere to find information, he'd give some interviews. That should be within the week—it seemed the connection to the Morel Corporation also expedited production times. The next step was finding office premises and hiring staff, because as soon as things went live, Si was hoping they'd have a rush of inquiries to deal with.

The office was a bone of contention between him and Lucien. So far, they'd agreed on pretty much everything, including logo design and color palette, taking turns to top, and getting up early for a workout and a run, but not on that. Si wanted the office to be in London, because he lived in London, and since he was the one who was going to be running the program day-to-day—once Lucien had trained him, of course—it made sense that the office was where he lived. Otherwise he'd have to *move country*.

Lucien wanted the office in Paris. His reasons were, in Si's opinion, utter bullshit, something about it being more central to most of Europe, cheaper to rent space—although only slightly—and closer to him as the executive consultant and Léo as the financial advisor. Si had argued that with modern technology they didn't *need* to be physically close, but after several conversations in which Lucien described London as a "cesspool," "horrific," and "unbearable," he'd sussed out the real reason.

Lucien didn't like London.

Leveraging his newfound friendship with Ben—he and Lucien had spent another weekend in Monaco just a few weeks ago, and Ben and Léo had met them in Paris for a couple of meals when Si was on one of his trips to meet with Lucien—he'd sent a quick text to confirm it. In fact, Ben had texted back that Lucien loathed London, with "loathes" all in capitals. He didn't seem to know why, though, just something about people and traffic and the weather.

It didn't really matter why; all that mattered was what he was going to do now. Si looked out the window of his Docklands apartment. He had a fabulous view, but more important, he finally had the damn place exactly the way he wanted it. While he'd been playing, and juggling studies with his already grueling schedule, the apartment had resembled nothing so much as a storage locker with a view. He'd spent the most time in the room he'd turned into a study, so it had been kitted out with everything he needed, but the other rooms had been barely furnished and... bare. After his retirement, he'd carved out some precious time to actually go shopping and unpack all his stuff, and now the apartment was *home*.

He'd really hate to leave it.

But Lucien wasn't wrong that office space was cheaper in Paris. And it *was* more central to other European countries.

Si sighed. Was he really going to move to Paris? He didn't speak French, for fuck's sake.

Maybe he could work remotely, at least for part of the week? Not initially, of course, but once they had the team hired and a rhythm going?

He picked up the phone and called Paul.

"*Bonjour*, Simon," the smooth-voiced Frenchman said. Si had been surprised when he'd met Paul—he looked rough-and-tumble, the kind of guy you might be tempted to cross the street to avoid, but he sounded like a languid aristocrat.

"Hi, Paul. Is the boss around?" The first few times he'd wanted to speak to Lucien after he returned to London, he'd called him directly. Lucien always answered, but usually just to ask if he could call him back. It didn't take Si long to wise up to the fact that he was interrupting meetings, and Lucien was, for some reason, not letting his calls go to voicemail as he did with others. He'd tried texting a few times instead, asking Lucien to call when he was free, but since Lucien always texted back, he was still interrupting, really.

Then he'd realized he could just call Paul. Paul always knew where Lucien was, and if he was in a meeting, whether that meeting could be interrupted, and—based on one conversation—whether Lucien wanted Paul to make up an excuse to interrupt a meeting so he didn't have to sit through it. So now Si always called Paul first—during business hours. The late-evening video calls he'd made to Lucien, he really hoped Paul didn't know about.

"He is in a meeting, but it should be over in the next few minutes. Then he has half an hour before the next one."

"Great—can you ask him to call me, please?"

"Of course." Paul made it sound like nothing would please him more, and Si decided to tell Lucien that however much he was paying Paul, he should add 10 percent.

"Oh, hey, maybe you can give me your opinion. Where do you think we should locate the office?" He was being cheeky for asking, he knew. Paul couldn't help but be aware that this was a source of conflict, since Lucien had asked him to put together a list of suitable properties in Paris, and Si had thrown a shit fit. Well, not exactly a shit fit. He'd expressed his dissatisfaction in an email to Lucien, cc'ing Paul.

In mostly capitals.

Paul's hesitation spoke volumes, and Si sighed. "You think Paris, huh?"

"It would be more cost-effective and convenient," Paul murmured. "I have lists of potential properties in both cities, and London is more expensive."

The weight of acceptance settled over him. At least if he lived in Paris, he and Lucien would be able to hook up more often. Four visits in six weeks and dirty Skype calls every other night just weren't enough. "Yeah. I don't suppose you know of any really good apps for learning French?"

Paul's laugh was surprised. "I will look into it," he promised, and Si grinned.

"Nah, don't worry. I'll sort it. Don't tell the boss I asked, by the way." There was no need for Lucien to know he'd already given in. Maybe he could use this to gain other concessions. After all, they needed to hire staff. What if they couldn't agree on who to hire? Si needed an edge.

He deliberately ignored the tiny voice that whispered that if he and Lucien hadn't established such a firm boundary between work and play, he could use it to gain *other* concessions.

"We are keeping secrets?" Paul asked, and there was a thread of humor in his voice.

"We are," Si confirmed.

"*Bon*. Oh—his meeting is just finished. Do you want to wait?"

"Yeah, that would be great. Thanks, Paul."

There was a click, and then the sound of boring hold music filtered down the line. Si wondered, not for the first time, who had decided that putting people into a coma while they were on hold was a good idea. In an effort not to fall asleep, he began making a list of things he'd need to do if he was going to move to Paris, even part-time.

It was not an exciting list.

Finally the music cut off and Lucien spoke, that accent washing over Si as it always did.

"Simon?"

"Hi, Lucien. Sorry to interrupt—busy day?" He didn't know why he bothered to ask. From what he'd seen over the past month and a half, when Lucien was working he didn't have anything *but* busy days.

Had it really only been less than two months since they'd met? It felt like they'd known each other forever.

"Average," Lucien said. "And your call is always welcome." He said it warmly, but in a scrupulously businesslike tone, even though Si liked to imagine there was a little something extra behi—*No no no! It's just sex. Just fucking.*

"You may change your mind about that," he warned, forcing his mind back on track. "I've rung to discuss the office site."

Lucien groaned. "Why will you not just concede that Paris would be by far the better choice?" The words were harsh, but Si knew Lucien well enough to recognize the energy behind them. His lover was keen for this battle, psyched for the challenge of convincing Si.

It was so fucking sexy.

No, it's not. For fuck's sake, you're getting weird.

"You've yet to convince me that it would be the better choice," he said calmly, adjusting his dick in his pants. *I can't believe that made me hard.*

They argued back and forth, both pulling out the same key points as before, neither willing to concede. Si was disturbed by how hot he found it. It wasn't even like he could say it was a tension-filled argument and his hard-on was a side effect of that. Their discussion was casual, filled with lighthearted insults and ridiculous points of attack. It was more *banter* than anything else.

Finally, Lucien sighed. "Simon, I have another meeting in ten minutes. We need to locate office premises as soon as possible. What will make you agree to site it in Paris?"

Aha! *Goal!*

"Well, while you have some good points as to why Paris would suit the program better, it's not as easy as me just agreeing," Si began, choosing his words carefully. "If the office is in Paris, I'll need to relocate. I have a home in London that I love, Lucien. I have friends here, and family. And I don't speak French."

"Details," Lucien said, and Si could almost see him waving a hand dismissively. "The nature of the program would have you working remotely part of the time anyway, promoting it and interviewing candidates, at least initially until we have enough traction to bring on more staff. There's no reason you couldn't work from home in London some days—perhaps Friday or Monday, or both? That would give you three or four days in England. It would depend on the week, and what was scheduled. As for not speaking French, you said you wanted to learn anyway, and how better than to be immersed in the language, surrounded by French speakers?" There was an edge of excitement to his voice, and Si smiled indulgently.

"I don't know," he said slowly, pretending to consider it. "If the office is in Paris, it's likely most of the staff would be French. I'd be working with people I have no common cultural background with." He cringed. That was pretty weak, really. There was no way Lucien wouldn't see through it.

The burst of laughter proved him correct.

"Very well," Lucien said, when he'd stopped chortling. "Allow me to make a suggestion. The office will be located in Paris, and you will have final say on staff hiring. Provided they are properly qualified for the roles and their references are acceptable," he added.

Si grinned. *Victory!* Even if it had been conceded.

"That sounds like a plan," he approved.

"Excellent." Lucien's warm tones made him feel as though he'd just achieved something far beyond the reach of mere mortals. "I will tell Paul to delete the list of London properties he thinks I know nothing about. When will you come to inspect possible sites? We should conduct interviews at the same time."

He didn't even have to look at his calendar. "I'll fly out day after tomorrow. Paul would have contacts at a recruitment agency, wouldn't he? We can contact them today and hopefully interview the day after I arrive."

"*Bien sur,*" Lucien agreed. "I will transfer you back to Paul?"

"Please. Oh, and Lucien, are you working late tonight?" Translation: how about some Skype sex?

The indrawn breath told Si that Lucien liked the idea. "No," he said. "I intend to be home at a decent hour."

"Good."

Chapter Eight

SI looked around the small office that would probably be his. At ten by ten feet, it was more than big enough to hold a desk, visitor chairs, and maybe a sofa or a small table and chairs. It also had a window—the view wasn't special, just of the buildings across the street, but at least there was some natural light.

The location was great, just a few blocks from the Morel Corporation headquarters, and the price was definitely right.

He wandered back out to the main office. There was a large reception desk already in place. The leasing agent had said it had been left behind by the previous tenants and was theirs if they wanted it. There was also room for several other desks, as well as a small area for visitors to wait. Next to the small office was a slightly larger one that could be used for meetings, and a kitchenette in an alcove.

Lucien was talking quietly to the leasing agent, but broke off when Si approached. "Well?" he asked, raising an eyebrow.

Si shrugged. "It meets all requirements," he said. They'd already decided that Lucien would handle the negotiations.

"Excellent." He turned back to the agent and said something in French. She smiled, then leaned closer to him and said something softly. Not that Si could have understood her even if he'd been able to overhear, since it had already been established that she didn't speak English and he didn't speak Fre— Was she *batting her eyelashes*? He'd thought that only happened in cartoons.

He strolled toward the door, torn between the desire to laugh and a few pangs of something he refused to call jealousy. After all, he and Lucien had decided from the outset, all those weeks ago in Monaco, *not* to pursue a relationship. They were just fuck buddies, right? So if Lucien wanted to flirt with other people, that was his business. Even if it did get Si's hackles up for some unknown reason.

I'm just horny, he decided. Sure, Skype sex and jacking off were great, but nothing was really as good as in-person sex with someone else. The car that had met him at the airport had whisked him into the city to pick up Lucien, and since then they had been working through Paul's list of properties with barely a moment alone. Si had hoped for some "private time" later in the evening, but maybe Lucien had other ideas? Crap, Si didn't even know where he was staying. He hadn't booked a hotel, just assuming he'd stay with Lucien, but that was pretty presumptuous, really.

"What are you doing?"

Si jumped and spun to face Lucien, who was looking at him curiously. He'd just been standing by the door, staring into space like a tosser for who knew how long. The flirty leasing agent was also looking at him, keys in hand.

"Just thinking," he blurted. "Not important. Are we done?"

The look Lucien gave him said he knew there was more to it than that, but he nodded. "Yes. Marie will send the paperwork to Paul today, and as soon as it is signed, we can move in."

"Brilliant," Si said, following them into the hallway. Marie locked the door, then cheerfully said something to Lucien, who responded politely. She turned a hopeful smile on Si. It was one he knew well, and he smiled his best public appearance smile back.

"Marie was wondering if she could have a photo and an autograph," Lucien told him, and even though his face was solemn, there was no mistaking the laughter in his voice.

"Of course," Si said, nodding, then as Marie delightedly rummaged through her handbag, he shot Lucien a glare that should have left him for dead.

Lucien snorted, then said softly, "I told her you were shy, but that blondes were your favorite."

As Marie exclaimed in triumph and raised her lovely blonde head, Si smirked at Lucien and said, "Oh, they are."

Maybe assuming he'd stay with Lucien hadn't been presumptuous, after all.

WITH his feet propped on Lucien's coffee table, Si closed his eyes and leaned back in the extremely comfortable chair that was twin to the one in Lucien's apartment in Monaco. "If I thought I could get it past the security guard, I'd steal this chair," he muttered.

Lucien chuckled nearby, and a moment later Si's hand was lifted and wrapped around a cold bottle. He cracked his eyes open and saw that it was his favorite brand of beer and that Lucien was taking a seat on the sofa, a glass of white wine in hand.

"How'd you know I like this one?" he asked, letting his eyes close again even as he lifted the bottle to his mouth.

"I pay attention," Lucien said. "That's also how I know that something upset you today."

Si shrugged. "I was just being stupid," he said. "It wasn't important, and I'm over it now."

"Are you sure? If moving to Paris is going to be a real—"

He opened his eyes fully, sitting up and putting his feet on the floor. "No. It's nothing to do with that, or the program. I was just... um, well... it's stupid. I feel like a fool for even thinking it."

Lucien looked at him expectantly, and Si sighed, his eyes firmly fixed on his beer bottle. "I was jealous. Marie was being all flirty with you, and it's stupid because we're just casual, but I was jealous. And then I started wondering if maybe I assumed too much by not booking a hotel, and... it just got dumber from there."

Laughter pealed through the room, and Si looked up, surprised. Lucien was laughing so hard, he had to put down his wineglass. Si reluctantly allowed a smile to tug at his own lips. A happy Lucien was impossible to resist.

"Are you laughing at what a dolt I was?" he asked, and Lucien shook his head and swiped moisture from his eyes.

"No," he said finally. "I'm laughing because Marie was flirting with me only because you don't speak French and she doesn't speak English. She was trying to convince me to act as intermediary between you." He picked up his wineglass and sank back into the sofa.

Si's jaw dropped. "What? Really? But she barely looked at me the whole time!" He felt even more ridiculous now.

Lucien shrugged. "I believe she was starstruck at first, but once she'd finished her sales pitch on the office suite, all she spoke about was you. She even asked me what your favorite food was." He smirked, and Si chuckled.

"I once said in an interview that I was looking forward to pizza at a friend's house that evening, and for the next week, I had pizzas delivered to my apartment night and day," he confided. "I really hope you told her you didn't know, because I don't think it would look good for the program if she started turning up at the office with food."

Shaking his head, Lucien huffed a laugh. "I do not know what your favorite food is, and that is what I told her. However"—his tone turned gleeful—"I did tell her that you are a fan of music that features whale song."

Si choked on the sip of beer he'd just taken. "You what?" he wheezed. Lucien merely smiled wickedly and sipped at his wine. "Cheeky bugger," Si groused, but it was kind of funny. Or it would be, as long as Marie didn't show up at the office with a Whales of the South Seas greatest hits compilation or something.

"As to the other," Lucien leaned forward suddenly, "yes, we have agreed that our… friendship is casual. However, I would not be so crass and rude as to make an assignation with someone else while in your presence."

"I wouldn't, either," Si said quietly.

"Also, until you find an apartment of your own—which Paul can assist with, by the way—you are most welcome to stay with me anytime you are in Paris. If that suits."

Si looked around the gorgeous apartment. It wouldn't exactly be a hardship to hang his hat there while he found something to rent. "Thank you. I appreciate that, it's very generous of you."

Lucien shrugged. "It is my pleasure—er, I did not mean—"

Si couldn't help but laugh at the tide of color that rose in Lucien's face. "I know what you meant. Although…." He wiggled his eyebrows, and Lucien snorted.

I SHOULD have known something would go wrong. It was all going too well. Si sat in one of the meeting rooms in the Morel Corporation headquarters, struggling to keep a neutral expression on his face as they interviewed another candidate for the bookkeeping role.

This was their third interview of the morning, and the last for the bookkeeper position. Next they had a two-hour break before the applicants for the administrator role arrived.

Si didn't think he'd last that long.

The morning had been a complete disaster. The candidates were all *terrible*.

Applicant one, a girl who barely looked old enough to have finished school, much less have the experience they'd requested: "Ohmigod ohmigod ohmigod, I am your *biggest* fan! I can't believe I'm actually meeting you, you're so *hot*! Can I touch you? Oh please, let me touch you!"

Or at least, that was what Lucien had later translated for Si. The entire outburst had been in rushed French, despite Lucien and Si having greeted her in English.

Lucien: Tell us about your experience.

Applicant One: (another barrage of French).

Lucien, with set face: (curt-sounding response in French).

Applicant One: (lunged from her seat to grab hold of Si and smash a wet kiss on his mouth before racing from the room).

Si had spent ten minutes scrubbing in the washroom before he felt clean, not helped by Lucien's explanation that apparently the girl was in fact a high school student who had seen the discreet ad placed by the recruitment agency, and because she was such a rabid fan of Si's had worked out that it was for the charity being rumored in the press. How she had gotten past the recruiter to earn an interview was something Lucien and Paul planned to find out.

Applicant Two, a distinguished-looking middle-aged man, had seemed a better option. His English was heavily accented, but comprehensible. Until they asked him if he had any experience working with charities.

Applicant Two, with lip curled in a sneer: "Charity? That is money wasted."

The interview ended there.

And now Applicant Three, a sharp-looking woman in her thirties, was answering Lucien's question about whether she liked football with a diatribe on the evils of organized sports. Since she'd practically been a lock for the role before that, Si was incredibly glad Lucien had made the casual inquiry. He couldn't stop himself from wincing as she declared that all athletes were sex-mad degenerates. Did she know he'd been a professional athlete? Was it better or worse if she did?

Lucien interrupted and thanked her for coming. As he ushered her out, he shot a look over his shoulder at Si that was both sympathetic and mischievous, and Si had a feeling he'd cop a lot of teasing in the near future about his "degenerate" status.

Or maybe Lucien planned to play on the "sex mad" aspect? That could be fun.

A moment later Lucien reentered the room, followed by Paul, who held a cordless handset and was dialing, a grim look on his face. He looked positively terrifying, his barn-broad shoulders set stiffly as he loomed over them—all six foot five of him. Lucien, on the other hand, seemed much more relaxed than he had been during the interviews, even winking at Si as he retook his seat.

"That was a nightmare," Si said bluntly, not sure why Lucien was suddenly so happy.

"Yes," Lucien said, shrugging. "But now Paul will fix it." He leaned closer to Si and lowered his voice as Paul pressed a button on the handset and ringing filled the room. "He takes it as a personal affront when things go wrong."

A glance at Paul had Si convinced that not only was the affront personal to Paul, but probably also to his entire family and all his ancestors. Si immediately resolved not to do anything to make Paul that pissed at him.

Someone answered the phone—in French, of course.

"Nicolas, Paul from Morel. I have Lucien Morel and Simon Wood here with me," Paul said in English.

His tone was icy, and from the pause at the other end of the line, Nicolas—whoever he was—heard it.

"Paul, Monsieur Morel, Monsieur Wood, how good to speak. Please excuse me my English. The interviews was good?"

Si inferred that Nicolas must be the recruiter Paul had used to find their applicants.

"The interviews were *not* good." Paul's response was knife-sharp. "I have never seen such poorly screened candidates in my life. If we wanted to interview random people, we would have collected them from the street." He never raised his voice, and his ire was entirely aimed at Nicolas, but Si was still glad for the bulk of the table between them. He raised an eyebrow at Lucien, who grinned evilly.

"*Impossible!* I select. They perfect for job," Nicolas insisted, his shock clear.

Paul flicked a glance at Lucien, who quickly and concisely described their experience with Applicant One. He was not even halfway done when Nicolas interrupted.

"*Excusez-moi*—Er, excuse me, monsieur, can you be speak more slow?"

"Tell him in French," Si said. The man would have enough to deal with, without having to translate as well.

"Are you certain?" Paul asked, and he nodded.

The conversation went fairly quickly after that, although of course Si didn't understand a word of it. Nicolas sounded fairly adamant, and Paul was implacable. Lucien said little, but watched and listened with an expression of intense amusement. It ended with Nicolas seeming to make assurances about something.

"Well?" Si asked.

Paul shook his head. "He says not only are those not the candidates he selected, they are not even among those he rejected. He has never heard those names before. He will make sure that this afternoon's interviews have been arranged with the right people, and will look into what happened." He smiled grimly. "It won't happen again. I am most sorry that your time was wasted."

Lucien waved a hand. "It was not your fault. This was Nicolas's warning, yes?"

Paul nodded. "If he does not correct the situation immediately, we will not use him again."

Wow. That seemed kind of harsh to Si, but on the other hand, after knowing Lucien just a couple of weeks he already knew he worked incredibly full days, starting before seven and often finishing the day with a business dinner. Paul had probably had to reschedule other appointments in order to clear this day for interviews.

"Shall I arrange lunch?" Paul asked. Si glanced at his watch. It was a little early still, but by the time it arrived… and if those hadn't been the "real" applicants, then they might need to fit in some more interviews this afternoon. He glanced at Lucien and shrugged.

Paul's phone rang, and all three of them turned their focus on it.

"You handle it," Lucien told Paul.

Paul picked up the handset and answered. The conversation that followed—in French, of course—was extremely frustrating for Si, because it mostly seemed to consist of Nicolas speaking and Paul murmuring agreement. There wasn't much that Lucien could even translate for him, although he did say that more applicants would be coming for interviews in the early afternoon.

Finally the call ended, and Paul turned to them with a satisfied expression. "This morning's interviewees were indeed the wrong candidates. The correct ones have been contacted."

"What happened?" Si asked. "I mean, how did we end up with the dregs?"

Paul snorted. "The dregs are exactly what they are. Over one hundred people applied for the roles, and Nicolas's assistant screened the applicants and only forwarded to him those who met our requirements. He then interviewed them and narrowed down the list to the ones who were supposed to come here today. He gave that list to his assistant to organize the interviews. She has an intern working with her this week, whom she thought could be trusted with so simple a task as calling to schedule appointment times, however the boy inadvertently accessed the wrong folder."

"You're joking," Lucien stated flatly.

"I wish I were. Needless to say, Nicolas assured me that his services are free of charge on this occasion."

Si inwardly cheered. The recruitment agency had offered them a discount because the Morel Corporation was an important repeat client, but their fee was still in the thousands per role filled.

Lucien's focus was elsewhere. "And I imagine he will not be taking on more interns any time soon."

Si just shook his head. "Did he send through the résumés of the new candidates?"

Paul nodded. "He has just emailed them to me. I will print them and bring them in, and then order lunch. What would you like?"

As Paul whisked around with his usual efficiency, Si hoped that the administrator they hired for On the Ball was even half as good as he was.

Although maybe a little less scary when pissed off, because Si was bound to piss them off at some stage.

THEY were nearly done with the interviews when Lucien got bored.

Si knew he was bored because he'd been the epitome of professionalism—as they'd both agreed to be—all day, but suddenly now he seemed to have an uncontrollable need to run his hand up Si's thigh.

Si ignored it.

Well, he tried to.

Okay, so it was bloody well impossible to ignore. He knew exactly what that hand was capable of, how it could make him feel, and having it so close to his dick, with the thumb stroking softly back and forth, played havoc with his nerves.

But the woman across the table was their best candidate for the administrator role, and she probably wouldn't want to work for him if he interrupted her to straddle Lucien and grind all over him.

So he did his best to shut out the distraction that was the tall, gorgeous blond beside him, and forced himself to focus on....

Bugger, what was her name again?

He snuck a glance at the résumé in front of him. Anna. That was it. He forced himself to focus on Anna.

Who was smiling faintly at him.

How long has it been since she finished talking?

It couldn't have been long, right? Lucien would have said something, surely.

Maybe.

Si smiled back at her. "I have one more question, Anna—are you a football fan?" After the morning's debacle, he'd made a point of asking all the candidates that, much to Lucien's amusement.

Anna laughed. "I am. In fact, I am very proud of myself for not demanding your autograph. I think I have been very restrained and professional."

"You have," Lucien affirmed with a grin. "Thank you for coming, Anna. It has been a pleasure to meet you." He stood, finally removing his damn hand from Si's leg, and showed her out. Si seized the opportunity to move his chair a little farther away. They still had to discuss which candidates they preferred, and he didn't want to risk more distraction. Lucien had promised him the final say, but that didn't mean he wouldn't try to talk him around.

Si had discovered that Lucien could be very convincing.

"You didn't have to rush her out," he said when Lucien came back. "I was going to offer to sign something for her."

Lucien paused momentarily, then finished closing the door. "I actually thought she was the one you wanted to hire," he replied, taking his seat, then frowning slightly when he noticed the new distance between them. "I didn't think she would need your autograph because when she's working for you, she'll be asking you to sign things all the time."

Si snorted. "Funny. So you think she's the one?"

Grabbing a pen, Lucien skimmed Anna's résumé again. "Yes. The others are just as qualified, but she has previous experience working with charities, and you seemed to get along with her a little better. Am I wrong?"

"No." Si almost wished he were, and that Anna hadn't been his pick, too. He'd been looking forward to exercising his final say. "You're right. She's the one I want."

"Excellent." Lucien made a note on a pad. "Now, what about the bookkeeper?"

Because of the schedule change and additional interviews, they hadn't had time to discuss the bookkeeper role before the administrator candidates had begun arriving.

"That's trickier," Si admitted. "I liked Michel—the second guy—but he doesn't have as much experience as the others, and none with charities." His gut was pulling him in that direction, but with no reasonable argument to back it up, he wasn't sure he wanted to follow it. If he'd been playing football he would have, no question—following his gut in the face of all logic had led to some of the best moments of his career. But this wasn't football, where a split-second decision under pressure could be excused if it went wrong. This was business, and he was supposed to use logic and reason. He needed to show he was capable of managing On the Ball in a manner that would convince his backers they'd made the right choice.

Wasn't he?

"That's true," Lucien said, staring off into the distance. A moment later he looked down and shuffled through the résumés and notes in front of him until he found what he wanted. "Why did you like him?"

"You mean for the job?" Si asked uncertainly. Lucien looked up and grinned.

"Yes, of course. I'm not accusing you of impropriety, Simon!" he teased.

Si slumped back in his chair. "Well, he was confident but not arrogant. He didn't interrupt while we were speaking or try to prove how much he knew,

but he answered all our questions without hesitating
or talking in circles. He'll probably have to deal with
a lot of teenagers with big egos and their parents, so
it's important he has the confidence not to back down.
He was easy to talk to, and he speaks French, English,
German, *and* a bit of Italian, which will probably
come in useful since we'll be working with so many
countries."

Lucien nodded. "I agree."

"You do?" Si blinked. "Agree that the languages
will be useful, or that Michel is a good candidate?"

"Both. The first woman had far more experience,
and the other man had worked with charities, but they
both spoke only French and English, and the man
didn't speak English that well. The woman also seemed
somewhat introverted to me, and as you said, teenagers
with egos and sports parents can be aggressive,
especially when they need money to play. Since this
will be a customer-facing role, we need someone who
can deal with the customers. I think Michel would be a
good choice."

Once again Si was faced with conflicting emotions.
He knew he should be pleased Lucien agreed with his
choices, but damn it, he had that final say card, and he
really wanted to use it!

"Okay then," he said, because what else could he
do? Lucien made another note on his pad.

"That only leaves one role."

Yeah. The one role they'd argued over on and
off since they'd met. Si planned to do a lot of the
interviewing and screening for the program himself,
but based on his research and projections, they would
probably receive more applications than he could
handle alone. Anna would do a lot of the preliminary

reviewing of applications, making sure all forms were filled in correctly and that there were no obvious points to disqualify the applicant—like not being eligible for a club team—and Michel would do the financial searches to ensure there was actually a need for funding, but somebody needed to properly read each application, and speak to coaches and trainers and the applicant themselves, to ensure that they were serious about developing their playing ability. Initially, there was also a need to visit around the clubs and make sure people knew the program existed and what it could provide.

Si would need help with that, especially since he was also supposed to be managing the program overall. The problem was who to hire. He wanted another former footballer, or a coach or trainer, someone who had experience on the ground, so to speak, and knew what to look for on the field. Lucien disagreed. Since the applicants would already need to be club eligible, he argued, there was no need to assess their ability, and thus an athlete was not necessary. Anybody with experience screening charitable applications would be suitable.

It had been a point of contention as explosive as the office location, and in fact the only reason they hadn't argued over it more was because they'd agreed the office took priority over staff. Although, once the office had been decided on, they still hadn't been able to agree, to the point that Paul had discreetly suggested that he hold off on advertising for the role.

But now it was crunch time. *C'mon, Si. Do this the logical way.*

"I have a specific candidate in mind," he said slowly. Perhaps arguing the benefits of hiring one particular person would carry more weight than arguing for a nonspecific entity.

Lucien raised a brow. "Oh?"

Si nodded. "Yes. Do you remember Tim Baker?"

Lucien's gaze sharpened. "He played with you for several years. An excellent player, although not as flashy as some." Si tried not to wince. Did Lucien think he'd been a flashy player? He wouldn't be the first one to say it. "He was also your teammate on the 2012 British Olympic team, and on the English team for the 2010 World Cup. Then he blew out his knee and retired. I haven't heard anything about him since."

"Right," Si said, pushing aside his insecurities. He *had* done some things on the field that could be termed flashy, but nobody had ever accused him of hogging the limelight, so he had to get over it. "Well, after he retired he had several more surgeries on his knee. Unfortunately, it wasn't the kind of injury that only prevented him from playing professionally. The damage he sustained means that even more than three years later, he still walks with a limp. His wife left him, although if you ask me that was no great loss. They never had kids, and his parents are dead, so he's basically alone except for some friends. He's been filling his time the last two years by volunteer coaching a community team for underprivileged kids, but I found out when I talked to him just after Easter that the funding's been cut for the program. Since he was volunteering anyway, he tried to get them to keep the team together, but without money for equipment and insurance, the local council's unwilling to do so." Si paused and drew in a deep breath. Lucien's face gave nothing away. "He has a bachelor's degree in business, and this isn't his first volunteer job. I think he'd be a really good fit for this role. He's dedicated to supporting underprivileged kids in the sport, he's smart, he knows football, and I'm pretty sure he'd be willing to travel. He was one of the few guys I've played with who didn't whine about it." Si stopped talking. He didn't want to ramble. He'd made his points, and now he needed to see what Lucien's response was.

Tim really would be great in the role, though. He didn't have any specific experience screening charity applications, but then neither did Si.

Lucien leaned back in his chair. "He does sound like an excellent candidate," he admitted finally. "I would prefer to have someone with charitable experience, but we are unlikely to find anybody who also has that level of dedication to developing youth in football."

"So…?" Si didn't want to assume anything, but it sounded like Lucien was in favor of Tim. Did that mean he wouldn't get to use his final say? *Bugger.*

"I would like to speak with him. We would have interviewed for this position anyway. You already know Tim, but I would like the opportunity to assess his suitability myself."

"Of course," Si said without hesitation. "I'll call and tell him about the position, and that we'd like to speak to him about it."

"He doesn't know?" Lucien's surprise was like a slap in the face.

"No! Of course not. We hadn't even advertised. Did you think I just went and blurted to him that I wanted him for the job without talking to you first?" His defensive tone was probably not logical and reasonable, but he couldn't help it.

"I apologize," Lucien said smoothly. "I did assume that due to your friendship you might have mentioned it to him. I should have known better." The formal words were at odds with the Lucien that Si had come to know, who defaulted to irreverent when around friends. Still, the sentiment was appreciated.

"Thank you," Si said stiffly, trying to let his resentment go. His ego had taken a real battering today, what with being called a degenerate and a flashy player and then essentially accused of unprofessionalism. *Accused? Exaggerating, aren't you, mate?*

Lucien reached out and caught hold of his hand. "I'm sorry," he said softly, gaze locked with Si's. Damn those blue eyes and their clear sincerity.

Si took a deep breath and let it out slowly. "It's fine," he said. "I can understand why you would think what you did. No harm done." And he meant it. It was a simple misunderstanding, but he'd let it get to him. He grinned at Lucien. "You'll just have to make it up to me later," he added suggestively.

Lucien laughed. "I have to check my messages and probably return some calls before I can leave. Why don't you call Tim, and we can rendezvous at the elevator in about half an hour?"

It was actually far more likely to be an hour or possibly longer, so Si said, "I'll call Tim and let you know what he says, and then if you're still busy, I'll go and shop for dinner for us, and meet you back at the apartment."

Lucien glanced at the closed door, then lunged forward and kissed Si, a quick kiss that was barely more than lips smacking together. While Si sat there blinking, wondering if it had really happened, Lucien stood and gathered his things. "I will let Paul know which candidates we are hiring. Thank you for organizing dinner. I'm glad you're here."

He left while Si was still trying to remember how to think in complete sentences.

"HEY, Si."

Si frowned. He'd never heard his friend and former teammate sound so down. "Hey, Tim. How's things?"

"Oh, you know. Same as always. Bit more interesting for you, though, Mr. Three-way." His tone brightened on the last, and Si chuckled.

"The online version of my life is much raunchier than reality," he said, "although there is something interesting in the works. That's what I wanted to talk to you about, actually."

Tim laughed. "Si, mate, you know I don't care that you bat for both teams, but it's not something I've ever wanted to try." Tim was one of the few people outside his family who knew for certain of Si's bisexuality.

"Nah, you're not my type," Si joked back, as he always did. "I like 'em better-looking than you." He leaned back in his chair, wondering if it would be too unprofessional to put his feet up on the table. *Yes, yes, it would be.*

"What's up, then, if it's not my body you want?" The lighter, breezier tone made Si feel a lot better. Even if bringing Tim into the program didn't happen, he had to make sure he called his mate more often. No way in hell was he going to lose Tim to depression.

"Well, you remember I used to talk about a nonprofit for—"

"Funding low-income kids to play football," Tim finished. "Holy fuck, mate, the rumors are true? You've got it up and running?" His excitement was clear.

"The official announcement goes out day after tomorrow. We're just waiting for the website to go live, and then On the Ball will be open for applications," Si confirmed, and just saying it aloud made him want to get up and do a victory dance.

"That's fucking brilliant, mate! Congratulations. I know you've wanted this for a long time." There was nothing but pleasure and pride in Tim's voice, no jealousy or despondency at all, which only reinforced for Si that he'd be a great choice for the program.

"Right? I've been working toward this for ages. I finally got my backers lined up, and the Morel Corporation loaned me an executive consultant—"

"Morel? Isn't that the name of the guy—ohhhhhhh. So the guy you're supposedly in a three-way with is actually a business contact?"

"Yes," Si said, and it was the truth, but his voice still cracked. *Damn it.*

Tim cackled. "Something you want to share, Si?"

"No," he replied firmly. "So anyway, Lucien Morel is the executive consultant for the program. Today, he and I were discussing staff hires, and I mentioned that you'd be perfect for screening and interviewing applicants. He'd like to meet with you."

Silence.

"Tim?" Had this been a mistake?

"I'm here," Tim said, and cleared his throat.

Oh. He was emotional.

"Is, ah, is that something you'd be interested in doing?" Si heard the hesitation in his own voice and wanted to kick himself.

Tim cleared his throat again. "Uh, yeah, mate. Yeah, I'd be interested. When can I meet with him? In Monaco?"

"Paris," Si said. "Oh, by the way, I'm moving to Paris. Our office is here and I'll need to be based here for most of the week too."

The snort of laughter was reassuring. "You don't speak French!"

"Believe me, I know. I've gotta get on that. Oh, hey, I forgot—you do!" Tim's uncle had married a Frenchwoman and moved to the French countryside—Si always forgot exactly where—so Tim had spent summers in France all through his childhood. He was pretty much bilingual.

"I do," Tim affirmed. "Would I need to move to France for this job?"

Si shrugged, then felt stupid because Tim couldn't see him. "Nah, probably not. You'd need to check in at the office every now and then, but most of your job would be remote. You're okay with traveling, though, right?"

"Absolutely. Though moving to France might not be a bad thing. Bit of a change, you know?" Already Tim sounded brighter, more interested in life. Si vowed to himself that his friend would get this job, no matter what he had to do to make it happen.

"Well, can you manage a flight to Paris tomorrow? I'm here for another couple of days while we get the office set up and put together the press release, so it would be a good time for you to meet with Lucien."

"Easy. I'll get online and book the flights now. And, Si? Thanks, mate."

Si pushed away the emotion that choked his throat. "Don't thank me yet. I plan to work you like a draft horse."

They ended the call laughing, and Si felt energized as he bounded out of his chair and got his things together. He'd ask Paul on his way out to clear time tomorrow for Lucien to meet with Tim, then he'd hit the supermarket and get something for dinner—steak, maybe. It felt like a steak day. He'd still likely beat Lucien home—

Bugger.

When had he started thinking of Lucien's apartment, that he'd only spent one night in, as *home*? *It's a reflex. End of the work day, going home. Never mind that it's not actually my home, that's just what I called it.*

Ignoring the little voice that whispered it wasn't so much the apartment that was home as *Lucien* was, Si slung the strap of his laptop bag over his shoulder and marched determinedly out of the meeting room and toward Paul's office. When he poked his head around the doorframe, Paul was on the phone, but gestured for him to come in. Si waited patiently while he wrapped up the call.

"My apologies for the delay," Paul said finally as he pressed a button to disconnect the call.

Si grinned. "You don't need to apologize to me because you're doing your job," he said. "If anything, I should be apologizing to you for adding so much to your workload." He winced, and Paul chuckled.

"And you're about to add more?" he asked.

"Yeah, I didn't actually realize how bad it was going to sound until I finished saying it. 'Sorry for adding to your workload, here's something else I need you to do.'" He shook his head, feeling like a dick, but Paul was grinning. The effect was a little disconcerting.

"Simon, this has been one of the most enjoyable months of my time here," he assured him. "Tell me what you need."

Si still hesitated, because really, what was enjoyable about rescheduling Lucien's appointments, but he really did need some time for Lucien to meet with Tim.

"Um, could you clear some time tomorrow for Lucien to meet with a prospective hire?"

Paul turned to his computer and tapped a few keys. He studied the screen intently. "How about at eleven thirty? I can organize lunch here if your meeting goes long. His next appointment isn't until one o'clock."

Relief settled Si's nerves. "Perfect. Thank you, Paul." He started to turn away, but was struck by a thought. "You don't happen to know a real estate agent for residen—" He stopped, because Paul had already turned to the table behind him and grabbed a manila folder from a file rack.

"I called an agent yesterday, and he sent over these listings this morning. If you don't like any of them, we can try someone else. His card is stapled to the folder if you have questions, or you can let me know, and I will act as intermediary."

Si opened the folder and flipped through the apartment listings, all of which looked great. He looked back up at Paul.

"One more question," he said.

Paul smiled. "Yes?"

"Is there any chance you would dump Lucien and come work for me at On the Ball? I doubt I can pay as much, and there's nowhere near as much prestige, but I can guarantee that you would be worshipped."

"Are you trying to seduce my assistant away?" Lucien's voice demanded, and Si jumped, then swung around to see him lounging in the doorway, a grin on his face.

"Bloody right," he retorted, and Lucien shook his head and looked over Si's shoulder at Paul.

"How many is that now this year?" he asked.

"Four," Paul said, with a touch of smugness.

Lucien raised an eyebrow at Si. "Paul and I have an agreement. He spurns all offers that would take him from me, and in addition to his usual annual bonus and benefits, I give him ten thousand euros per job offer he receives."

Si's jaw dropped. *Ten thousand euros?* And he'd already gotten four job offers this year? It was only the end of June!

"I know *exactly* what Paul is worth," Lucien said cockily. "I could not run my office—and probably my life—without him."

Turning back to Paul, Si sighed. "It seems I can't afford you," he said, and his mournfulness was only partly put on.

Paul winked. "I would say I am disappointed, but you just paid for my trip to Argentina next year," he replied, and Si laughed.

Lucien came into the office and dropped a file on Paul's desk. "Have you spoken with Tim?" he asked.

Si nodded. "Yes, and Paul has just cleared some time for you to meet with him tomorrow. I'm off to the supermarket now. Steak okay for dinner?" As the words left his mouth, he realized how very *domestic* they sounded, and shot a worried look at Paul. Lucien's assistant was focused on his computer screen, and when Si looked back at Lucien, he smiled and shook his head slightly.

Oh, right. Paul deals with sensitive shit all the time. As much as Lucien is paying him, he must be like a vault. Still, he had to be more careful, especially with the press release about to go out. There could be no

insinuations that he'd gotten the funding for On the
Ball by sleeping with the Morel heir.

SI was still thinking about discretion and how it applied
to him and Lucien when Lucien got home nearly two
hours later. In that time, Si had gone to the supermarket,
decided to do chips with their steak, as well as veg—
nothing was ever as good as fried potato—and spent
some time peeling and cutting potatoes ready for frying.
He'd also made sure to open a bottle of the red wine
Lucien liked best with steak, and that had gotten him
thinking about whether it was odd for him to know such
a random detail. After all, he and Lucien hadn't know
each other *that* long, and a lot of their time together
had been virtual and not physical. Wasn't knowing
which wine a man liked with his steak the kind of fact
reserved for family, longtime friends, and partners?

The monotonous task of preparing the potatoes
gave him plenty of time to think about that. Was he
getting too close to Lucien, emotionally? The guy
made a great mate, and the sex was brilliant, but they'd
agreed upfront that they didn't want anything else. Si
was, technically, still in the closet about his bisexuality,
although that was really just about the lack of an official
announcement more than anything else. Was now really
the time to come out? There was so much going on, so
much riding on his reputation—the world had become
a lot more accepting over the years, but was he willing
to risk On the Ball without knowing for sure which
way the wind of opinion would blow? Discretion still
seemed the best option, and since he could never ask
a boyfriend to live in the closet with him, that meant

keeping things the way they were. Even if Lucien was kind of fantastic and would make a great boyfriend.

The sound of the front door closing dragged him out of his thoughts. "Simon?" Lucien called.

"In the kitchen!" Si turned on the burner under the frypan of oil he had on the stove, and then the one under the pot of water for the veg. Lucien came in, smiling.

"Oh, what's this?" he asked, sounding intrigued.

"Steak and chips," Si told him, putting a heavy *duh* tone in his voice. "And steamed vegetables, because we're not animals."

"Good choice."

Was it dumb that the note of approval made Si's insides warm? *Not dumb. Dangerous.*

Lucien poured himself a glass of wine, got Si a beer—which he'd just been about to do himself, damn it—and wandered off to change out of his suit. When he came back, Si was just putting the chips in the hot oil.

"What can I do?" Lucien asked, and Si tossed him a smile. Fancy that, the Morel heir helping in the kitchen. Si knew Lucien could cook, of course, had watched him do so several times, but it still tickled his funny bone to see it—especially when it came time for the washing up.

"In a couple minutes, you can put the veggies in the steamer," he said, indicating the small pile of chopped veg on a cutting board. "And then watch the chips while I do the steak."

Lucien huffed. "I don't think so. I have seen how you English cook steak, and I would prefer not to eat shoe leather this evening. You watch the chips, and I will cook the steak."

A sharp pang of annoyance hit Si. He knew how to cook a bloody steak, thank you very much. Sure, the

English as a rule didn't have a great track record with steak—his mum was a great example of that—but that didn't mean *all* Brits were incapable of cooking it properly.

Lucien kissed him on the cheek. "You can cook the steak. I know you are a good cook."

Shit, was he being that obvious? Worse, was he actually upset about who cooked a couple of steaks? How utterly ridiculous.

Si laughed, mostly at himself. "Nah, you do the steak. I started the potatoes, I may as well finish them."

Lucien smiled at him, blue eyes warm, and something settled in Si. They pottered around the kitchen together, cooking dinner, chatting idly about silly things like the oil Si was using for the potatoes, and how he hadn't liked the selection of steak at the first supermarket he'd gone to, so he'd tried another. In truth, he would have preferred to go to a butcher, but hadn't been sure where to find a good one nearby. That started a friendly game of one-upmanship over who had the better local butcher, which continued throughout their meal. Si eventually conceded defeat, both because his butcher in London didn't make organic maple-flavored sausages, and because he'd soon be moving to Paris and Lucien's butcher would likely become his butcher anyway, so it seemed silly to keep arguing.

After they'd cleaned up, which was pretty easy with the top-of-the-line dishwasher and cookware Lucien had, they settled in front of the TV, Lucien in his favorite chair—only because Si hadn't managed to beat him to it—and Si on the couch. First they watched the last half of a documentary on climate change, and then a sitcom that Si found deadly boring. He had to force his eyes open several times, until finally he just gave up and let himself drift off into dreams.

And what amazing dreams! He was lying on the beach on a tropical island, the hot sun beating down on him while the *swoosh* of the waves acted as nature's white noise machine. He was warm, comfortable, and relaxed... and someone was sucking his dick.

Someone with a very talented mouth, who knew exactly what he liked.

Si tried to lift his head to see who it was, but for some reason he couldn't, and really, who cared? He was so hard, throbbing, and he instinctually knew that whoever this person was, he knew them, trusted them—and they were incredibly good.

The hot mouth left him for a moment, and a wet tongue licked across his balls. Si moaned, and the sound of his own voice broke through the dream and woke him.

But someone was still nuzzling his sac. He looked blearily down at Lucien, who had a wicked smile on his face, and felt sleep clear rapidly.

"Hello, Sleeping Beauty," Lucien murmured, dropping a kiss on the tip of Si's cock, and Si sputtered a laugh.

"You're supposed to kiss my mouth, idiot," he chided. "Anyway, fancy yourself a prince, do you?"

Lucien shrugged as he got to his feet. "I had to wake you somehow, and why not with an adults-only fairy tale?" He held out a hand. "Let's go to bed. I have plans for you."

Si glanced around the room. The TV was off, and the place was tidy. He'd noticed that about Lucien—despite having a daily housekeeper, the man never went to bed without tidying up after himself. *He'd be a dream to live with.*

Shaking that thought out of his head, Si tucked himself somewhat painfully back into his pants, then took Lucien's hand and got up. They strolled hand in hand through the apartment to Lucien's bedroom. Si was hard as a pike, but the leisurely pace was a delicious tease, if somewhat uncomfortable.

When they (finally) reached their destination, Si raised an eyebrow. The bedside lamps were on, casting a soft glow over the room. The bed was turned down, and a bottle of lube and a condom were ready on the nightstand. "Look at all this effort you've gone to," he teased, and pulled off his shirt. Lucien grinned and just stood, watching him as he stripped off his pants next. After spending so many years of his life in locker rooms, Si was used to being part- or fully naked in front of other people, but he still felt that having Lucien watch him strip should probably make him self-conscious. It didn't.

"Come on, catch up," he coaxed, leaping onto the bed. It was a great bed, firm enough to give proper lumbar support, but with a pillow top that felt like sleeping on a cloud. Si had already decided that when he moved to Paris, he was getting a bed just like this.

Moments later, Lucien slid naked into bed beside him, and their mouths met halfway, just a moment before their bodies. Si couldn't help it, he moaned, and in his arms Lucien shivered. For long moments they just lay there, kissing, luxuriating in the delicious sensations of warm, hard flesh and hot, wet mouths, until finally Lucien broke the kiss.

"You're topping tonight," he murmured. Si smiled and kissed the sensitive skin behind Lucien's ear, that place that always got a reaction.

"Okay."

They were both vers, and had had a great time over the past weeks switching things up and discovering each other's preferences. For example, Si now knew that Lucien particularly liked to bottom when he'd been dealing with a stressful work situation and wanted to give over control.

Which meant tonight, Si was in charge.

He kissed Lucien again, then one more time, just because his lips were so irresistible, and then pulled away. It was tempting to go back for yet another kiss, to indulge in the sensation of Lucien's skin against his and the puffs of their mingled, panting breaths, but it was time for him to take control. "Hands and knees," he ordered, and a thrill went through him when Lucien complied. He spent a moment just admiring the long, smoothly muscled line of that back, the curve of his ass. And all that golden skin. Really, Lucien should just stay naked all the time.

Grinning at the thought, he ran a finger lightly down Lucien's spine, loving the shudder of reaction. Lucien was so sensitive to touch—he loved being stroked and petted, even in a nonsexual way. Si fitted his hand over the very tempting globe in front of him and squeezed gently, skimmed a finger oh-so-lightly around his pucker, then glided his palm back up toward Lucien's neck.

Lucien looked over his shoulder at Si. "Really? You're going to tease me?"

"I love teasing you," Si told him solemnly, but he dropped a kiss on Lucien's asscheek and reached for the lube.

The whole time he was prepping Lucien, he stroked him with his other hand. It was a deliberate combination of gentle, soothing touches along his back and wicked, twisting fingers in his ass—first one, then two, and finally three. Lucien's breathing grew more and more ragged, until finally he was moaning with every touch, gasping Si's name with every movement of Si's hands. Si himself was so hard he could barely focus. Every twitch of Lucien's muscles shot through him like fire, yet he felt almost like he could have predicted every tiny reaction; he'd never in his life been so attuned to a partner—and more, *wanted* to be. Wanted to know exactly what he could do to bring forth each gasp, each moan. Every sound from Lucien made Si feel like a superhero.

They'd had dirtier sex, more active sex, but this slow tease, this exploration of sensation, seemed… more. Si was so intensely aware of Lucien, of his every reaction, of how he *felt* under Si's hands, against his body, and by the time he finally rolled on a condom and pushed into his ass, the connection between them was so intense, he nearly came on the spot.

From the way Lucien clenched around him, he wasn't far off himself. Si's body wanted so badly to pump, to thrust, to enjoy the hot clasp of Lucien's ass around him until he came, satisfied, but he forced himself to go slow. To glide in and out. To fully appreciate every millimeter of friction, every nerve ending. To glory in the tight heat encasing him. He paused, savoring the sensation of Lucien around him, of the hot, damp skin of his back under Si's palm. That glorious, velvety, golden skin. He bent his head and blew lightly, loving the way gooseflesh prickled and Lucien shivered.

"Simon, Simon," Lucien moaned, thrusting his ass back toward Si. "Please, more. Now. Harder." The words were like tinder to a flame, and Si's control broke.

He thrust hard, and Lucien's cry of triumph rang in his ears like music. What felt like hours but was more likely mere moments of thrusting later, Lucien came with a shout that probably disturbed the neighbors, his ass clenching around Si like a vise and pulling him over the edge. He collapsed against Lucien, barely maintaining the presence of mind to wrap his arms around him and roll them to their sides.

For a long time they just lay there, panting. Si knew in some part of his brain that he should be trying to regain his faculties, but it just wasn't happening.

"You're a tease," Lucien finally said, his breathing still uneven. Si smiled.

"Yeah."

Silence.

"We should definitely do that again."

Chapter Nine

LUCIEN sat back and listened to Simon and Tim bickering over who to approach to help them run the training camp, smirking slightly. The two were obviously old hands at arguing with each other, often knowing where a sentence was going before it was completed.

It had taken him only a few minutes of conversation with Tim to know he was the perfect person to help Simon with screening applicants. He'd told him so, offering the job to the sound of Simon's quickly cut-off victory yell.

Since then, the two former athletes had seized the ball and run with it, so to speak. Paul had ordered in food, and over lunch the conversation had focused on what steps were next, and how to prioritize them. The press release was due to go out within twenty-four hours, and they were expecting requests for interviews from sports journalists shortly after—and if the requests didn't come, Simon and Tim had some key contacts they could lean on to make them happen. But before those interviews, they needed names. Names of former athletes and football professionals to draw people to their mini training camp.

Simon had spent the morning contacting people, and they already had an impressive list, but nobody that he was willing to hand over management of the camp's training program to. Originally, he'd wanted to do it himself, but Lucien—backed up by Tim—had pointed out that during that time he would still need to manage On the Ball, as well as coordinate the camp overall and be available to any press that showed up. Somebody else was needed to run the programs and oversee the coaches. Tim had declined as soon as Simon had looked at him, before he even opened his mouth to ask, claiming he wasn't bossy enough. That had led to twenty minutes of debate that Lucien wisely stayed out of.

"Right then, that's settled," Simon said now, drawing Lucien's wandering mind back to the table. "I'll call him this afternoon. He's a bloody good coach, and we'll be lucky to have him. Are you sure he's been bored since retirement?"

"That's the rumor," Tim confirmed.

Lucien glanced over at the notepad in front of Simon, saw the name written there, and smiled approvingly. He was indeed a good coach, and a high-profile one. He was also known for his charitable works, so it seemed likely he would agree, although Lucien and Léo had approved a small stipend for the camp manager.

"All right, then. Gentlemen, I am afraid I must leave." Lucien stood, and Simon glanced at his watch.

"Crap, I hadn't realized the time. Okay, we'll just hammer out a few more details, and then I'll take Tim to the airport."

"It was a pleasure meeting you, Lucien," Tim said, standing and offering his hand. Lucien shook it warmly. "And thank you again for the job."

"That is my pleasure," Lucien assured him. "And please remember that if you ever change your mind about the salary, there will be no hard feelings." Tim had very generously waived a salary, claiming he had enough money invested from his football career to keep him comfortably, and that the funds would be better spent within the program. Lucien had reservations about that, but could not refuse such an offer—although he would ensure Tim's employment contract covered all bases.

Their discussion began again before he'd even left the meeting room, and he grinned as he headed for Paul's office. He'd check in, then prepare for his next meeting, which sadly had nothing to do with football.

It was quite a shock to walk into Paul's office and find his father there. Usually Édouard stuck to his own offices on the top floor, mostly because employees had been known to become nervous if he wandered freely through the building. After the time a finance assistant had spilled a cup of scalding coffee over himself and his computer, resulting in a trip to the hospital for burns treatment—and a new computer—the executive team had decided it would be safer for any visit by Édouard to be planned and "leaked" well in advance.

Lucien and Paul were an exception to this, of course, but still Édouard did not visit often, and when he did, it was usually in Lucien's own office.

"Lucien, there you are," his father said, rising from the chair he'd been ensconced in while he read... was that the file Lucien needed for his next meeting?

"Here I am," Lucien affirmed. "As are you."

Édouard smirked. "Relax, son, I am not here to interfere—or send you back to Helsinki, although I believe it's really rather pleasant there at this time of year. You weren't in your office, and I knew Paul would know where I could find you."

Lucien shot Paul a grateful smile. Paul could indeed have directed his father down the hall to the meeting room he'd been in, but instead had allowed Lucien a few extra moments to enjoy his break.

"Was there something you needed, or just the pleasure of my company?" he teased, and his father snorted a laugh.

"Your mother would like 'the pleasure of your company.' She mentioned yesterday that she has not seen you for some time."

Lucien did a quick calculation and realized with some surprise that it had in fact been over two weeks since he'd last seen his mother. Usually he tried to see her at least once a week—it kept her from poking into his life.

"I will have to rectify that immediately, won't I?" he said, mentally running through his schedule. Breakfast the next morning was out of the question, since Simon was still staying with him, but lunch was a distinct possibility. "Thank you, Father."

"Don't thank me yet, I'm still here." There was a decided twinkle in Édouard's eyes. "Tell me, how is the charity project coming?"

Édouard's personal interest in the project surprised Lucien. His father was generous to charities, but Lucien had never known him to show any interest beyond allocating funds.

"Very well," he replied, somewhat cautiously. "We have secured offices and hired staff. The press release goes out tomorrow, and we expect it to be well received."

"Excellent. And Mr. Wood? I hear he has been in the building the last few days, setting everyone aflutter."

A light clicked on. Édouard was fishing for information about Simon, probably as a result of what had happened in Monaco. "I don't know about that, but he's certainly here. I just left him a few moments ago." Lucien regretted the words the moment they left his mouth. His father's face lit up.

"Well, I should go and say hello! Where is he?"

Lucien cast a desperate glance at Paul. "Er, he has someone with him, one of our employees, and they are due to leave shortly—"

"Then I had best go now. Which room?"

Lucien was considered one of the most astute and fast-thinking businessmen in Europe, but whenever he went up against his father, he was left feeling like a bumbling teenager. Unable to conceive of a reason not to, he told Édouard which meeting room, and then after he left, slumped into a chair.

"Why does that always happen to me?" he asked, directing the question not so much at Paul as at the universe.

Paul answered anyway. "Because he's your father and all fathers have the ability to make us feel like

children again. Here are the notes for your meeting."
He handed Lucien the file Édouard had been reading.
Lucien took it and flipped through, not really seeing
anything.

"Thank you. Could you please make sure Simon
and Tim are… not hijacked by my father for too long?"

Paul only smiled.

LUCIEN strode into his mother's favorite bistro, five
minutes late for their lunch date. The hostess recognized
him and smiled in greeting.

"Good afternoon, Monsieur Morel. Your mother is
here already. Please follow me." She led him across the
room, inquiring politely how his morning had been. He
answered just as politely, and then as she left wondered
if maybe he should have asked about her morning.

Damn Ben.

"Hello, Mother." He leaned down to kiss her, then
took his seat.

"Hello, Lucien." The warm tone of her voice
always made him feel loved. His parents weren't like
those he'd seen on television programs while growing
up, always involved in every aspect of their children's
lives, but he'd never doubted that they loved him. "You
have been busy lately." The subtle remonstrance made
him glance up from his menu and chuckle.

"I apologize for neglecting you," he said. "I have
been very busy with a new project, but that is no reason
to forget my loving mother."

She laughed, and waved a hand. "You have always
been impudent."

He grinned at her. "So, what have you been up to?"

As his mother updated him on the latest goings-on in her life—which took quite a while, since she'd always been extremely active socially—he scanned the menu and wondered idly how Simon was doing. He had been due to return to London this afternoon, but had decided to delay until they saw how the press release was received. After all, he might be needed in the office.

Speaking of the press release.... Lucien glanced at his watch. It had now been sent out. They would know soon if they would need to pull strings to get the press coverage they wanted.

"Lucien, are you listening?" his mother demanded, and Lucien blinked and focused on her.

"Of course I am," he told her, injecting just the right amount of indignation to his tone. Quickly, he thought back over what she'd been saying. Absorbing conversations without actively listening was a skill he'd inherited from his father, and one that drove his mother insane.

She frowned prettily at him, trying to appear stern. "What has you so distracted?"

The waiter appeared right then, giving Lucien a moment's reprieve as they ordered drinks, but the moment the man left, he was once again in his mother's sights.

"I'm sorry, Mother. I was thinking about the project I've been working on. It goes public today."

His mother lifted a brow. "The football one?"

Lucien's surprise was genuine. "Father told you about it?"

She waved a hand dismissively. "Of course, months ago."

Another shock. "Well, that's more than he told me."

"Perhaps he wanted it to be a surprise," she suggested, tongue firmly in cheek, and Lucien laughed.

"Perhaps," he agreed. "Regardless, we've worked quite hard to get it up and running in such a short time, and I'm anxious to see what the response will be."

His mother reached across the table and took his hand, her eyes soft. "Lucien, if you have worked hard on it, it would not dare be anything but a success."

Once again, that feeling of being loved enveloped Lucien.

"Thank you, Mother."

She patted his hand, then withdrew hers to her side of the table. "Now, tell me what is happening between you and Simon Wood."

Damn.

He should have known she'd know.

"I don't know what you mean," he replied, shrugging. "Simon is running this project—as I'm sure you know, since you seem to be so well-informed on the topic. He and I have worked closely the last few weeks, and will probably continue to do so until things are firmly established." He took a sip from his water glass.

His mother gave him *the look*, the one that had young socialites scurrying to do her bidding. When he'd been a child, that look had been enough to have him confessing all his sins. Even now he fought the urge to squirm.

"I heard that he's staying with you." It wasn't a question, but Lucien knew he was expected to respond nonetheless.

"Yes. We've been working long hours, and we get along quite well. I didn't see a need for him to take a hotel, not when there's so much room in my apartment. He's begun looking for an apartment, however."

The waiter approached just then to take their food order, and Lucien was glad for the reprieve, even if he knew his mother wouldn't let it go.

Sure enough, the moment they were alone again, she raised an eyebrow and said, "You have never invited any other business associates to stay with you."

He forced a smile. "I think Simon and I are friends, now. We have many common interests. Believe me, Mother, we both feel strongly that there can be no hint of impropriety regarding the Morel Corporation's funding of this program." There, that was suitably vague, but his mother should take the hint.

Her gaze sharpened, and she took a sip from her wineglass. "Nobody who knows you would *ever* accuse you of impropriety in business, Lucien. But, I see your point. Now, tell me, how are Malik and Léo, and Léo's charming boyfriend—Ben, isn't it?"

LUCIEN went directly from lunch to the On the Ball office. It would make him slightly late for a meeting, but he needed to take a few minutes to see how things were, if the press release had been a success.

As he climbed the stairs—he could have taken the elevator, but he hadn't had much opportunity to exercise lately and the stairs would do him good—he thought about how much his life had changed lately. He'd always loved his work, enjoyed the mental acrobatics needed to operate in the top tier of the business world, but each project, each challenge, had just been an exercise on paper, with the end goal merely profit. On the Ball was different. He felt different working on it— more excited, more energetic.

Or maybe that was just working with Simon.

Lucien sighed. He couldn't deny it. Their relationship was supposed to be purely casual, just business and friendship, but it was becoming increasingly obvious to Lucien that his feelings for Simon weren't casual. He'd suspected as much for several weeks, but had brushed off his instincts—after all, he hadn't known Simon that long and most of their contact, with the exception of a few short visits, had been online or by phone. Nobody could form deep feelings that way. Could they?

It seemed that it his case, he could. If his growing need to see or speak to Simon often hadn't been enough of an indication, the stab of annoyance he'd felt when Simon told him he'd be looking for apartments in Paris was. Why did Simon need an apartment? He could stay with Lucien. Except wealthy adult men who were just friends didn't share apartments. That was what boyfriends did.

So… did he want to take that next step with Simon? It was so damn complicated, especially now, with the launch of On the Ball and the substantial financing the Morel Corporation had contributed. If Lucien and Simon began publicly dating, they potentially opened the program up to negative publicity—because people were always looking for ways to find fault, even when there was none. On the other hand, if Lucien and Simon didn't date publicly, Lucien was essentially consigning himself to living in the closet again—and worse, because his social position required him to attend certain events with a date, there would be a large element of deceit involved.

He sighed again as he reach the correct floor. He didn't know what to do, but he knew he wanted to do something. Friends with benefits wasn't going to be enough for him for much longer. Maybe he should just take a bold step.

The phone was ringing as he stepped through the main door to the office. Anna had the receiver wedged between her shoulder and ear as she tapped away at her keyboard, and Lucien made a mental note to ensure she got a headset of some kind.

Ten feet away, Michel was also on the phone, and through the door to Simon's tiny office, Lucien could see that he, too, had a phone pressed to his ear.

And yet the ringing continued.

Should he... do something? Everybody was clearly busy. What should he do?

Making a snap decision, he crossed the room to the desk that would be Tim's when he was in the office, and swept up the handset of the phone there.

"Hello—er—On the Ball," he said, immediately wondering what he was supposed to do next. Fortunately, the caller was from a local newspaper, asking for an interview with Simon. He knew how to handle that, and shortly thereafter had taken the man's details and assured him that Simon would call him back for a short phone interview.

By the time he hung up, Simon had come out of his office, a huge grin on his face. For the moment, the phone seemed to have stopped ringing.

"Hey! Did you see?" Simon gestured to where Anna was still on the phone, a stack of message slips beside her. "The phone's been ringing off the hook since the press release went out. At this stage, it's mostly still the press looking for more information, but their interest has been positive, and some of the news and sports sites have already uploaded short articles.

Plus, at least three news programs that I'm aware of included a mention in their noon reports."

"That's wonderful," Lucien said, smiling, a little weight lifting off his chest. They'd been prepared to artificially stir media interest if necessary, but this was so much better—and easier. Still, he should warn Simon.... "You know there will be some negative coverage, too? People trying to boost ratings and their own publicity by making nasty comments?" It was a sad reality.

Simon shrugged. "Yeah. We'll ride it out, if we have to." His mobile rang, and he glanced at the screen. "This is the TV interview I was hoping to tee up. I've gotta take it." He swiped the screen and lifted the phone to his ear as he turned back to his office. Lucien watched him go, aware that he was smiling for no real reason, and then turned to catch Anna's gaze on him. She smiled.

"Will you be here long enough for me to put you to work?" she asked, and Lucien started and looked at his watch.

"No, I'm already late. I shouldn't even be here, I just wanted to see how things were going," he admitted, heading for the door. He paused at the threshold. "Is there anything I should know?"

Anna shook her head, just as Michel hung up his phone, crowing in delight. "One of the biggest youth leagues in Italy would like a meeting with Simon."

Lucien left the office with a huge grin.

Chapter Ten

EVEN though he knew it was happening, it was still somewhat of a shock when Lucien flipped through the satellite TV channels to Sky Sports News and saw Simon being interviewed. He'd flown back to England two days before to do this interview and others, and seeing his face sent a pang through Lucien that he refused to acknowledge. If he did, he might have to do something about it, and that could be disastrous.

So he turned up the volume and sat back in his favorite chair to watch the interview.

Simon was a superb face for the program. He was an engaging speaker, enthusiastic about On the Ball, and had a clear rapport with the interviewer, a veteran sports journalist. They discussed the program's aims, the kind of support it could offer, and the upcoming "showcase" training camp, which Simon was quick to invite viewers to inquire about. Then the interviewer said, "I understand that most of your funding is coming from the Morel Corporation, and that Lucien Morel is heavily involved in the program. Your headquarters are in Paris. Are you concerned that as a result, people may perceive the program as being primarily French?"

Lucien groaned and gulped back some wine. What a stupid question, clearly designed to plant just such a thought in people's minds and stir controversy. He picked up his phone to make a note for Anna to make sure On the Ball's PR company came up with something to balance it.

On the TV, Simon was speaking. "... actually a brilliant question," he was saying, and nothing about his tone or expression said that he was being sarcastic. If Lucien hadn't known him so well, he would have assumed he meant it. "I wish I'd thought of that argument when Lucien and I were debating where to locate the office. I wanted London, but in the end, France was friendlier to our budget and more centrally located. Italy and Germany were also considered for those reasons, but ultimately we decided against them purely because of language. I only speak English, you see. Tim Baker—I think I mentioned that he's part of our team—is fluent in French, and Lucien is fluent in English, so with both of them helping I'll be able to get by until I learn the language myself. In any of the other countries, Tim and I would have had to deal with a language barrier from the get-go."

The interviewer appeared to consider this. "That makes sense," he said finally. "What about your funding?"

Simon grinned widely. "That was amazing luck. I already had commitments from several grant programs, and of course I was investing myself, but I had several large European companies on my list to approach. The Morel Corporation happened to be the first appointment I could get, and Édouard Morel completely blew me away with his generous offer. He was quite excited about it, actually—" Lucien snorted. "—never before supported a recreational charity, but as he pointed out, the Morel Corporation has offices and interests in every EU country. The Morel Foundation already endows charities in those countries for food, shelter, and education, so the next logical step is recreation and professional development."

Lucien sat up straight and put his wine down, the thumb of his other hand already dialing Paul. His phone rang before he could finish, his father's name flashing on the screen.

"Good evening, Father," he answered, somewhat distracted by what Simon was saying—something about the Morel Foundation's work in the Czech Republic. "I'll have to call you back, I'm—"

"You're about to call Paul in a panic and have him ensure we have a PR statement ready regarding our involvement in your program," his father interrupted. "I too am watching Simon's interview. We do, by the way. I had it drafted after I saw you earlier this week."

Lucien sank back in his chair. "Why?" he murmured. "And thank you. I should have thought of it."

"When I was speaking to Simon and Tim, we discussed possible responses should the size of our contribution come up—which it has. Simon and I agreed that it would be politic to emphasize Morel's European interests. The comment about me being excited was completely his invention. I don't recall being excited in the slightest."

Huffing a laugh, Lucien thanked his father again and ended the call. On screen, the interviewer was asking Simon about him. Simon nodded enthusiastically.

"The original business plan for the program called for the hire of a management consulting firm. I know football, and I've got the education to manage this program, but I've never had any practical business experience on this scale—I don't think managing my personal finances counts. I was determined that everything would be done right, not mucked up because I didn't know what I was doing, but from the beginning, when I researched the fees those companies charge, it stung. It was enough to put three kids through the program every year. Édouard recognized this, and offered Lucien's time and expertise as an additional donation from the Morel Corporation. I was happy to accept, knowing that we'd be able to put that money to better use, and that Lucien is an excellent executive consultant—better than we would have been able to afford otherwise. It also turns out that he's a rabid football fan." Simon shrugged, as if that was surprising. The interviewer nodded with an "oh, really?" expression on his face. "So Lucien has been really helpful in getting things set up. It's great to be able to call him when I have a question, and he was able to give me a list of common pitfalls people experience when applying for all the licenses we needed, which helped me avoid them. Who knew ink color could be so important?"

The interviewer chuckled, and Lucien smiled proudly. With those last two sentences, Simon had cast Lucien into the role of distant advisor. He should have known Simon would have the situation in hand;

he'd always seemed particularly adept at dealing with the media.

The interview came to a close, and Lucien flipped the channel to the business news. His phone rang again, but this time it was Léo.

"Did you see the interview?" Léo asked.

"Yes. You did too?" Lucien responded, lowering the volume of the TV and picking up his wine again.

Léo chuckled. "I was planning to watch it anyway, but Ben insisted. He said we had to be informed."

"Informed about what?" Lucien asked. "And if he wanted information, why didn't he just ask us?"

"I don't know, to both questions. It went well, though. I always worry about live interviews." The underlying note of relief in Léo's voice reflecting what Lucien was feeling.

"So do I. I almost advised him not to appear on this program, but it's so popular, we really couldn't turn it down." The program focused solely on football, and had a huge audience throughout the UK and Ireland. Right now, hundreds of thousands of people had just heard all about On the Ball, and would hopefully discuss it with their friends, neighbors, and colleagues.

"Of course not," Léo agreed. "What I really called for, though, was because Ben and Dani have been watching social media for mention of On the Ball, and Ben says it's doing really well. There are the usually prophesiers of doom, and some catty comments about the photos in Monaco, but those are mostly being shouted down. Interest has been growing rapidly over the past several days, but right now, commenters are saying that the website is slow."

"We can fix that," Lucien said. "It's a good sign—there must be a lot of visitors. Thank you for letting me know."

"Ben would have called himself, but he's using his phone to monitor Twitter." Léo's voice was bone dry, and Lucien laughed as he ended the call.

Quick calls to Paul and Anna set his mind at ease. They were already aware of the issue and working with the site host to fix it.

Lucien went to prepare himself some dinner. He was just finishing his meal when his phone buzzed with a text.

Busy?

He smiled.

That depends on what you would like.

He reread the text with smug satisfaction before sending it. His written English had greatly improved since he'd met Simon and they'd started "sexting"—a word he hadn't know existed before.

The phone rang.

"Did you see the interview?" Simon demanded, barely giving Lucien time to say hello.

"I did. I was very surprised by some of your comments, but my father called and assured me the two of you had planned it together."

Simon laughed. "Your dad's brilliant. When he came in the other day I nearly shat myself, but then he started hatching plots. By the time he left, Tim was convinced that world domination was on the horizon."

Lucien propped his feet on the coffee table, something he'd only started doing recently, and only when he was alone. "It may be in his long-term plans. I haven't read all of the latest corporate forecast yet."

He smiled as Simon laughed again. That sound was addictive. "Are you at home?"

"Yeah, finally. I feel like I haven't been here in a million years, and I only get one night before I move on. The publicity in the UK is done for now, and tomorrow I head to Italy."

"When is the meeting with the youth league?" Lucien tried to remember Simon's exact itinerary. He had quite a few interviews set up with the Italian media, and meetings with several of the football clubs, but the youth league meeting was what excited them the most.

"Day after, at three."

The very scarcity of his reply told Lucien that Simon was nervous about the meeting.

"You're ready for this," he assured him. It was true. The league had assured them that they would have an English speaker on hand for the meeting, but Simon had decided to hire a translator anyway, just in case. He'd ensured that the person he hired had at least a basic knowledge of football, and had already spoken to the translator at length about the information that would need to be conveyed, and the kind of questions to expect. The translator, who had been recommended by Paul from his magical directory of contacts, had called Paul to say he'd never been so thoroughly briefed for a job, not even when he'd worked with the United Nations.

"I know," Simon said, but there was a note to his voice that left Lucien unconvinced. He decided a change of subject was in order.

"The seminar I had scheduled for Friday has been canceled," he said. "I told Paul not to backfill that time. I thought perhaps I could meet you in Italy and we could spend the weekend being lazy tourists." He found himself almost holding his breath in anticipation of Simon's response—because, of course, a weekend in Italy together was the sort of thing couples did. It would be a big step for them, and his suggestion had essentially been a declaration that he wanted to develop their still very new relationship beyond friends who had sex.

Which he did.

He wasn't sure when Simon had become such a huge part of his life. They hadn't known each other that long at all, but the time when Simon had been staying with him had been like a puzzle piece in his life—one he hadn't known was missing, but that had slotted into place perfectly, completing the picture. It had felt so natural that he hadn't even realized it was happening until Simon left on the publicity tour, leaving Lucien to roll over in bed, reaching for someone who wasn't there, or turn to make a comment to someone while watching television, only to find the couch empty.

He'd even considered getting another chair made, so he wouldn't have to share his—and wasn't that foolish, since Simon was looking at apartments to lease.

But Simon's celebrity status, especially now, did call for discretion, and Lucien understood that. He didn't want to do anything to jeopardize On the Ball. So while part of him waited anxiously for a response, most of him knew that it would likely be no.

"God, that sounds amazing," Simon moaned. "When can you get there? On Friday I'll be in Venice. My last interview is at four, and then I was going to fly back to Paris for the weekend right after, but I can change my flight and just go straight to Budapest on Monday morning. A weekend in Venice with you is like a dream come true."

Something lodged in Lucien's throat, leaving him momentarily unable to respond.

"Lucien?" Simon sounded uncertain, and Lucien forced himself to swallow the lump.

"Yes," he said, and if his voice was husky, it must be because of allergies. "I will go to the office on Friday morning and make certain my desk is clear, then fly to Venice sometime in the afternoon." Léo had an apartment in Venice, which he had bought years ago when he and Malik had spent a summer there. Lucien knew that with a single phone call, he and Simon could have a beautiful place to stay overlooking the Grand Canal.

"Brilliant," Simon enthused, the uncertainty gone. "I can't wait. Let me check the name of the hotel for you."

"No. In fact, you can cancel the hotel. Léo has an apartment we can use. It's beautiful, far nicer than any hotel. And more private."

Those last words hung between them.

"Are we making a mistake?" Simon asked at last, and Lucien felt it like a fist to the gut.

"I am not," he said carefully. "Our personal relationship"—such cold words to describe what was between them—"has no impact on our professional one. I would not welcome the media attention in my private affairs, nor should it be diverted from the good On the Ball can do. That is the only reason I suggest discretion." He winced and slumped down in his chair. He sounded like an arrogant, pompous fool.

Simon chuckled. "Sometimes I forget about the silver spoon you were born with, and then you go and say stuff like 'my private affairs.' All right, Luc, I'm in this with you. Discreet, but together."

The relief that swamped Lucien left him struggling to form sentences. "Luc?" was all he managed to say.

"Yeah. It was that or Luci, and I like the *K* sound better. Have you never had a nickname before?" The amusement and warmth in Simon's voice washed all the tension from Lucien's muscles. He couldn't believe that just a few words in a certain tone could make him feel so much more at ease.

"No one would dare," he proclaimed, reaching for the wineglass he'd abandoned earlier. "I have always been Lucien."

"Really? Even as a little tyke?" The surprise in Simon's voice was a little more than Lucien felt the situation warranted.

"Always," he reiterated, sipping his wine, wondering how he felt about the idea of Simon giving him a nickname. Maybe if it was just Simon, it would be okay, but he didn't think he wanted everyone to start calling him Luc.

"So, even when you were just a tiny little miniature with untidy blond hair—I'll bet it was almost white when you were a kid, wasn't it?—and big blue eyes, everyone called you Lucien? Your mum or whoever didn't have a pet name for you?" He was teasing now, and Lucien relaxed even further, feeling a level of warmth and comfort heretofore unknown. The only thing that could make this conversation better was if Simon was in the room—or maybe even squeezed into his chair with him.

Lucien considered the idea. No, the extreme comfort of the chair would be negated by having two people crammed into it. But they could cuddle together on the couch.

"I have never been called anything but Lucien," he replied, tickled by the idea of his childhood nanny ever giving him a nickname. The woman had been efficient, kind, and even affectionate at times, but had raised him quite formally. He deliberately ignored the comment about his hair having been untidy, although it *had* been white-blond until he reached school age.

"Well, first time for everything. A nickname will keep you humble, my nan always said." Simon paused. "Although I'm not sure how that works, exactly."

Lucien chuckled. "Your humility-granting nickname is Si, yes? I heard Tim call you that."

"Yep, and that's how I mostly think of myself. Although my sisters sometimes call me Si-Si, and let me tell you, when I was a teenager, hearing that called out in public took me right past humble to humiliated." He was laughing, his adult self mocking his teen insecurities.

"I can imagine," Lucien said, grinning as he filed the knowledge for future use. "Do you mind that I call you Simon and not Si?"

There was a pause, and the mood changed slightly. "I don't mind," Simon said slowly. "I mean, it is my name. Is there a reason you don't want to call me Si? Nicknames are often used between people who are… close."

That was not an easy question to answer, although he had brought it on himself. Lucien inwardly cursed himself for killing the fun.

"It's not so much that I don't want to call you Si," he said honestly. "I think in the future"—hell, should he be mentioning the future?—"I will very possibly use your nickname. But I have always thought of you as Simon, and so there is an adjustment to be made… also, people close to you call you Si. I think I like the distinction of being close to you, and yet calling you Simon." Did that even make sense, he wondered dismally. "It's foolish, I'm sorry."

"No, it's not foolish," Simon replied quickly. "I think I get it. It's part of the reason why I decided to give you a nickname, really." An awkward silence sat between them. "And somehow we've managed to kill this conversation by talking about our *names*. That has to be worthy of an award, right?"

Relieved, Lucien laughed outright.

Chapter Eleven

SI glanced again at the address in Lucien's text. It seemed the water taxi was at the right place, but motherfucking *wow*. He was right on the Grand Canal and hardly more than a stone's throw from St. Mark's Square. Lucien hadn't been wrong when he'd said Léo's apartment was "well-situated."

He paid the driver, then clambered out of the boat and onto the small dock, hauling his bag with him, and called Lucien.

"Are you here?" his lover asked, actually shocking Si. He'd never heard Lucien answer the phone so informally.

"Standing at the door," he replied when he could find the words. He heard movement through the phone, then a moment later the grand door before him opened, and there was Lucien.

Si's instinctive grin was mirrored on Lucien's face. Although they spoke daily and texted in between calls—sometimes on business, mostly not—Si's crazy publicity schedule promoting On the Ball meant it had been almost three weeks since they'd seen each other, and the ache of that had sat on Si's chest like a lead weight. Was he being stupid, he wondered, to have fallen so far and so fast? Probably, but he wasn't willing to give up his time with Lucien just to be sensible.

He should probably start thinking about coming out. Lucien's private life wasn't plastered over the tabloids, but he was openly bisexual, and it was unlikely he'd want to go back into the closet for Si's sake. And Si wouldn't want him to—in fact, the only reason he hadn't come out during his playing career was because there hadn't been anybody in his life worth the media bother that would have followed. He'd never really dated seriously—there was always too much else going on, and nobody, man or woman, had intrigued him enough for him to want to rearrange his schedule to include them. Would things have been different if he'd met Lucien back then?

Yes.

He pondered that as Lucien grabbed his overnight bag and hauled him into a small but lovely foyer. Seconds later, the front door was firmly closed, and Lucien's mouth was on his.

Mmmm.

He'd missed this so damn much. He wrapped his arms around Lucien, sliding one hand up into that immaculate blond hair. Si would never admit it aloud, but he deliberately messed up Lucien's hair whenever he could. He loved seeing his usually impeccably tidy lover all mussed and knowing it was because of *him*, that *he* was allowed to rumple Lucien and see him in this less-than-perfect state.

Finally they broke apart, panting. With more than a little satisfaction, Si took in the flush of color on Lucien's cheeks, the way his blue eyes glittered, his messy hair. He'd done that.

"Let's go upstairs," Lucien said, his voice husky, accent thick. "Most of the residents are not here, but this is still a shared space."

Si gestured toward the rather ornate staircase. There was probably a lift somewhere, but a couple flights of stairs would do him good right now. "After you." Wow, was that his voice? When had it gone all growly like that?

Probably about the time Lucien squeezed your arse, mate.

They jogged up three flights of stairs, and Si winced a little when he realized his panting was not all due to their kisses. He really needed to get back into a proper workout routine. At least Lucien was huffing a bit more than him; he couldn't have borne to be more unfit than a stuffy businessman.

Finally Lucien was opening a door, and Si followed him inside, desperate to (catch his breath) get his lover's pants off.

Fuck me.

"Whoa." He stopped short. "You weren't joking when you said this place was beautiful."

Lucien, still breathing heavily, smiled and closed the door. "You've met Léo. He has impeccable taste."

That was for sure. Momentarily postponing sex, Si wandered over to the french doors, taking in the opulent chandeliers and luxurious furnishings, and stepped out onto a balcony overlooking the Grand Canal. The summer sun shone brightly. He felt Lucien step up

behind him and leaned back just enough to touch him—
and the tension from his hectic week disappeared.

They stood in silence for a long moment, just
basking in the warmth and taking in the view. Finally,
Si turned his head.

"Going to show me the bedroom?"

WHEN he felt Lucien stir beside him, Si wondered
how he had the energy. They'd been going at it for
hours, and Si himself felt like a wet rag—in the best
possible way. He just wanted to lie in bed and drift
off to sleep beside Lucien. Although come to think,
something to eat wouldn't go amiss.

"Simon?"

Si forced his eyes open and focused on the hot
blond propped on an elbow beside him. "Hmmm?"

"How did the meeting go yesterday with the youth
league?"

"I already told you it was good," Si mumbled,
letting his eyes drift closed again. The bed shifted, and
then Lucien's lips drifted across his left cheekbone. He
smiled reflexively, even though there was no way in
hell he could get it up again just yet.

"But what does 'good' mean?" Lucien murmured,
now nibbling on Si's ear. That tickled a little, and Si
swatted at him gently.

"Stop that. There's no way you can be ready to
go again." He opened his eyes and looked right into
Lucien's amused blue ones.

"I just like touching you." He suddenly looked
very vulnerable, and drew back a little. "If you—"

"Don't go anywhere," Si interrupted quickly. "I
like it too." It made him feel warm inside.

Lucien smirked. "Good. Now, about the youth league...."

Si sighed. It really had been a very positive meeting. He didn't know why he was so reluctant to talk to Lucien about it.

Except he did.

"They were very enthusiastic," he said, a decided lack of enthusiasm in his tone. "We spoke at length about what On the Ball hopes to achieve, and the ways we plan to implement the program in Italy. They have their own financial support program, of course, but it's quite limited, and they said that based on what we discussed, they would be very happy to encourage those they can't help to apply to us."

"That's wonderful," Lucien said, his eyes narrowed. "So why are you so unhappy about it?"

Si heaved a sigh, and sat up, only just avoiding a collision between his and Lucien's skulls. "One of the board members kept making comments. Nothing really overt, but he mentioned the fracas in Monaco, then later said something about how you and I must be good friends. And other than that, he was very quiet, but he hardly took his eyes off me, and I don't think it's because he thought I was sexy." He tried to laugh, but it was halfhearted at best. "It was... odd."

Lucien leaned back against the headboard, a thoughtful expression on his face. "That must have been uncomfortable for you," he said, taking Si's hand. "I think he must be extremely homophobic, to the point that even a rumor is enough for him to pass his flawed judgment."

Slumping beside Lucien, Si nodded. "Yeah. I guess we're lucky the rest of the board was at least ignoring the rumors." There was a heavy, sinking feeling in his stomach.

"No, I think it will not matter." Lucien's tone was contemplative. "Our publicity has been better than we anticipated, and applications are much higher than we expected. Enrollment to the training camp, also. Anna told me it will be full soon. These are all signs that this program was desperately needed. I have never been secretive about my bisexuality—I am not so publicly visible as you, but the gossip sites have reported me dating both men and women. There have always been rumors about you. And there was, as you say, the fracas in Monaco. I think people don't care. They can see that our private lives have nothing to do with the management of a necessary charity."

Pursing his lips, Si wondered how to answer that. Perhaps Lucien was still high on sex?

"That's the most naïve thing I've ever heard you say. If I didn't know better, I'd say you're drunk."

Laughing, Lucien leaned over and kissed Si's cheek, then got out of bed. "I will admit that last part is perhaps wishful thinking, but I do believe people have weighed the rumors against what benefit On the Ball will bring, and have decided they want the charity." He strolled, naked, toward the bedroom door. Si watched his flexing back muscles with something approaching awe. "Are you hungry?"

AS they lingered over brunch the next morning on the terrace of a charming and not-too-touristy restaurant, Si and Lucien amused themselves with people watching. Si felt only slightly ashamed that they were making up stories about the varied people who passed, and not always nice ones. After all, it wasn't as if any of the people would ever know.

"Henpecked husband," he declared, his eyes on a man walking apace with his female companion.

"You always say that," Lucien complained. "Why can he not be her assistant? Or bodyguard?"

Si looked at him and raised an eyebrow. The man in question did not look fit enough to guard anything. Lucien chuckled and conceded.

"In this case you are probably right. But I maintain that your last henpecked husband was not one."

"This conversation is so weird," Si mused. "Do you want more coffee?" He glanced around for the waiter.

Lucien didn't answer, and Si turned back to see him staring quite fixedly at something. "Luc?" He followed his line of sight, and his jaw dropped. "Wow."

The most stunningly gorgeous couple he'd ever seen was strolling along the street. Both were tall, the woman around six feet, the man well over. Both had clear muscle tone, although not so much as to be bulky, and were beautifully dressed to show their assets: fit young bodies, money, and class. That alone would have garnered them plenty of attention, but when you added their sheer good looks.... Both were wearing sunglasses, but that didn't hide the flawlessly smooth tanned skin, the glossy black hair—long and flowing down the woman's back, immaculately cut and styled for the man—the sharply angled cheekbones (both), full lips (hers), and action-hero square jaw (his).

Silently, Si and Lucien watched the couple pass, their gazes tracking every step. Once they'd gone far enough that watching further would mean craned necks, they turned back to look at each other.

Lucien cleared his throat. "Well, that was...."

Si huffed, and reached for his water glass. "Yeah." He shifted slightly. Both the man and the woman had had a sway to their walk that was... stimulating. "I think we need more coffee."

Murmuring agreement, Lucien gestured to the waiter, and then they sat in awkward silence until Si couldn't hold it in any longer.

"Did you see—"

"Wasn't her—"

They both stopped, stared, and then laughed.

"Are we going to shamelessly objectify those poor people?" Si asked as their waiter brought the coffee.

Lucien made a noise that for anybody else would have been a snort. "Those were the Walkers, from New York. They have come to Europe at this time every year for the last five years, and go to London, Paris, Monaco, Rome, Venice, and Prague, always in that order. I dated a woman once who is a personal friend of Claire Walker, and she told me they have clothing designed specifically for these little promenades. I'm sure they're hoping to be objectified. The final effect is certainly worth the effort."

"You know them?" Si asked, surprised. "You should have said hello." He grinned. "It would have given me the chance for a better look at both their arses."

Grinning, Lucien mock-shuddered. "I don't know them beyond casual acquaintance, but that is enough for me. They are more fun to look at than talk to." He tossed back his espresso in the Italian way. Si had never gotten the hang of that, much preferring to sip his coffee. "Their arses are amazing, though," Lucien continued, his tone reminiscent. "I once saw them at the beach in Nice."

"Was he shirtless?" Si asked, picturing it and trying not to salivate.

Lucien raised an eyebrow. "They both were."

Si almost swallowed his tongue. He'd forgotten about the whole topless thing—it had been a while since he'd been to the beach in southern France—but imagining the couple lying side by side, oiled up, their beautiful bodies on display....

The sensation of Lucien's hand over his brought him back from his daydreams, and he met that amused blue gaze. "Should I feel abandoned?" Lucien inquired. Si turned his hand and gave Lucien's a quick squeeze before letting go and standing. He wished he could prolong the moment, maybe even hold Lucien's hand properly as they explored Venice, but anything more than a brief touch could be noticed and sensationalized on social media.

"Not at all. In fact, I need you now more than ever." He winked and Lucien also rose. "It's all well and good to look at pretty people, but I know who I want to spend my time with. Besides, it's not like you're so hard to look at," he teased, pulling enough euros out of his wallet to cover the bill.

"Thank you," Lucien said, although there was a faint wash of color on his cheekbones. "I'm glad we can talk about this. Some of my—" He faltered. "Some of the men I've seen in the past were not comfortable with me admiring others, especially women. And the women felt the same, about men."

A curious thrill ran through Simon. Has Lucien nearly called him his boyfriend? *Idiot, you are his boyfriend. Well, all but officially.*

"I'm not jealous like that," he said, skimming over the rest. "As long as it's only looking, who cares?

Besides, how often do you see a couple who both have so much appeal?"

Lucien grinned. "Every year, about this time," he joked, and they wandered off toward the apartment.

Chapter Twelve

THE strident ring of his phone brought Lucien to full consciousness. Beside him, Simon stirred and muttered, but didn't open his eyes.

Sighing, Lucien heaved himself to a sitting position and squinted at the clock beside the bed. Two thirty in the morning? Something had to be wrong.

He stumbled out of bed, groaning, and staggered to the dresser across the room where he'd left his phone. It stopped ringing just before he got there—of course— but then started again immediately.

Uh-oh.

He swept it up and answered with only a cursory glance at the display. "Malik? If you're drunk-dialing—"

"Shut up and listen," his friend said urgently, and Lucien woke up the rest of the way. "A friend of mine at

Bonjour Celeb just called me. There's an article about you in tomorrow's edition."

"Why do you have friends at that rag?" Lucien asked, not quite understanding. He may not like it, but gossip rags did occasionally publish articles about him. It came with being wealthy.

"Lucien, pay attention. The article is about you and Simon. Apparently there are pictures."

Stomach cramping, Lucien looked sharply toward the floor-to-ceiling windows. They were two floors up, but someone with a telephoto lens and access to a building across the canal could still get photos. *Fuck.*

"What kind of pictures?" He strode back to the bed and shook Simon's shoulder.

"Not that kind—sorry, I didn't think. She said you were holding hands in some, walking close together in others." Malik sounded genuinely apologetic, and Lucien sank down to sit on the bed, relief making his knees weak. It still wasn't ideal, but….

Simon was awake now, sitting up and looking at Lucien worriedly.

"It's Malik," Lucien told him. "*Bonjour Celeb* is publishing an article about us tomorrow, with pictures of us holding hands." The gut-punched expression on Simon's face said all that was necessary. "Malik, I'm putting you on speaker." He pulled the phone away from his ear and tapped the icon.

"Hi, Malik," Simon said, and if his voice was a little more than just sleep-roughened, none of them commented on it. "What do you know about the article? Is there any way we could get them to pull it?"

"Simon, I'm so sorry," Malik said. "My friend waited to call me until after the paper had been put to bed. She knew Lucien—and you—would have the clout to maybe stop it. It's too late now."

"Not your fault," Simon muttered, taking Lucien's hand and gripping tightly. "How bad is it?"

"Mostly conjecture," Malik told them. "They have pictures of you both there in Venice, some with you holding hands—those are the ones they've played up. From what she told me, the article mentions Lucien's bisexuality, references rumors of you being bisexual, and says you've had plenty of opportunity to get close lately, working on the program. She said they had a few 'sources close to' quotes, but since they don't outright say you're bisexual or that you and Lucien are seeing each other, I don't think those people are terribly close to either of you."

Lucien sighed. The article itself sounded like the usual drivel, but those pictures... most straight men didn't walk around Venice holding hands.

"Thank you, Malik. I'm going to call my father and Morel's PR director. If any press calls to ask you questions—"

"No comment," Malik replied. "Or I'll just hang up. I'm going to call Léo and Ben now and warn them."

"Thank you," Simon said. "And thank you so much for calling. We might not be able to stop it, but at least it won't blindside us over breakfast."

Lucien ended the call, and they sat there on the bed for a moment, staring at each other.

"I have to call my father," Lucien said finally. "But first we need to know what we're going to do."

"What do you mean?" Simon asked blankly, and Lucien wondered if maybe he was in shock.

"We can issue separate statements denying everything."

"Don't be stupid!" Simon snapped. "They have pictures of us holding hands, Lucien!" He sucked in a deep breath. "I'm sorry. I just…. This isn't how I wanted to come out."

Lucien remained silent, unsure what to say, and Simon squeezed the hand he was still holding.

"I'd kind of started planning it. I was going to come out for you. It was… it was going to be a declaration of how I feel about you."

The words hung between them. Lucien was torn between being elated and heartbroken that Simon wouldn't get the moment he'd wanted.

"You're still coming out for me," he said huskily, and Simon heaved a sigh.

"Yeah." He smiled weakly. "Not quite the same way, but I guess when our grandkids one day ask how I told you I love you, this will make a great story. 'Well, kids, a trashy gossip rag printed a photo of us holding hands.'"

Forcing himself to swallow past the lump in his throat—what did he address first, love or grandkids?—Lucien chuckled. "And then you made a joke about our grandkids, and I found out you love me." He glanced down at the bed, just to make sure it was still there, because he felt like he was floating.

Simon looked stricken. "Oh hell, I really bollocksed that up, didn't I? What I mean to say was, Lucien, I love you. I know we haven't known each other that long, but—"

Lucien placed his free hand over Simon's mouth. "Stop. No qualifications. I love you." He felt Simon's lips move against his hand as he smiled, and he grinned in return.

IT was several hours later before Lucien had the chance to jump in the shower. Ideally, he would have liked to get a few more hours sleep, but there was no way his nerves would let it happen.

Me, nervous. How astounding.

He'd woken his father, who had in turn woken the Morel Corporation's director of PR. The four of them had discussed the various options open to them and had settled on a simple statement that said he and Simon were seeing each other, their relationship was still new, and they were taking it one day at a time.

Guy Vernon, the director of PR, had drilled Simon very thoroughly on what the press might or might not know about him. The rumors had been around for years, but were unconfirmed. Had anyone ever asked outright if he was gay or bisexual?

"No," Simon had replied. "I'd remember if they had, because I wasn't going to lie. I didn't want to say anything that might one day bite me in the arse."

"That's astonishing," Guy marveled. "All those rumors, and no reporter ever just asked? Well, it's fortunate for us. If people want to know why you never told them you were bisexual before, just tell them nobody asked. The rumors were all there, and you just assumed people believed them."

It seemed a little slippery to Lucien, but it was the truth, so while people might speculate and doubt, there was nothing concrete with which to cast aspersions on Simon's integrity.

So now they just had to wait. Guy had the statement prepared, ready to send out as soon as the news hit the streets—which would be very soon now. They'd considered sending it out sooner and preempting *Bonjour Celeb*'s headline, but decided that smacked too much of a cover-up.

They'd woken Tim, Anna, and Michel to warn them. The On the Ball offices weren't open on Sunday, but Simon insisted it was courtesy to let their employees know they might be facing a shitstorm on Monday morning. Plus, somebody had to talk to the web host to make sure their site could handle increased traffic—just in case.

Lucien got out of the shower, toweled off, and dressed. He didn't bother with shaving or further grooming. He wasn't planning to leave the apartment all day. He and Simon had considered returning to Paris that morning to face the media uproar from there, but as Guy had pointed out, it wouldn't change anything. They had made arrangements for one of the Morel planes to take Simon to Budapest the next day, though, instead of him taking a commercial flight. The executive airport had much better security, and they were accustomed to keeping paparazzi at bay.

Léo had texted while they were talking to his father and Guy, and had assured them the apartment was theirs as long as they wanted it should they decide to stay on in Venice. He'd also sent the number of a "very good and discreet" local firm that could provide security and run errands for them, and offered round-the-clock service. Lucien had already called them and arranged for groceries to be delivered ASAP, and for security—which had arrived forty minutes later. There was currently one guard in the foyer of the building, and one outside the apartment. Both were well over six feet, built like tanks, and had long and distinguished military records.

Sighing over the need for guards simply to spend time with his boyfriend, Lucien walked out into the main room. The first rays of sun were peeking around the tightly closed curtains. It would have been nice to open them, but wasn't worth the risk of a telephoto lens.

Simon was unpacking a bag of groceries.

"Oh good, they came," Lucien said. He'd expected swift and efficient service, but also knew it could be difficult to find supermarkets open this early in Italy.

"Yes, and they're very good," Simon replied. "The fruit and veg and pastries are really fresh, and everything else is exactly what we asked for. I wonder if the company has a branch in Paris."

Picking up a still-warm brioche, Lucien broke it in half and lifted a piece to his mouth. Not quite as good as the ones from his favorite patisserie at home, but still excellent. He offered the other half to Simon.

"I've already had one, thanks." He grinned, and while it was strained, Lucien was still relieved to see it. "I couldn't wait for you. They smelled too good."

"Did you make coffee?" Lucien asked, although the lack of coffee smells would indicate no.

Simon shook his head. "Sorry, I was too busy scarfing down pastries."

Chuckling, Lucien crossed to the cupboard beside the stove and pulled out the cafetiere. There was an automatic coffee machine, but he'd found over the years that there was something soothing about the process of making espresso the traditional way. He didn't often take time to do it at home, but when it Italy, it made for a nice change.

Part of him knew that by occupying himself with mundane morning chores, he was avoiding the drama that loomed on the horizon. More, he and Simon were both avoiding having to talk about it.

He made the coffee as Simon finished putting away the groceries and plating the remaining pastries and some fruit. They settled at the dining table and exchanged trivialities as they ate, the lulls between sentences becoming longer and longer until they finally lapsed into silence. Lucien racked his brain for something to say. He was a highly educated man, knowledgeable on many topics, well read, current on all major social and political issues, as well as informed about the arts, sport, and any number of other topics. He was widely considered to be an interesting and amusing conversationalist.

And right then, he couldn't think of a damn thing to say to his lover, the man he loved and planned to spend his life with.

His phone rang, and they both jumped and gasped. Simon began to laugh. There was an edge of hysteria to the sound, and Lucien glanced at him in concern as he swiped the phone up from the table and glanced at the display.

"Ben," he said, and answered it, putting it on speaker. "Good morning, Ben."

"Is it?" his friend said darkly. Lucien heard street sounds in the background. "I'm looking at the cursed headline."

Lucien was touched. Ben had clearly not gone back to sleep after Malik had called, but instead had gone out at this ridiculously early hour, when Lucien knew he was not really a morning person, to get information for them.

"How bad is it?" Simon asked.

Ben sighed. "It could be worse. The article is mostly bullshit, but there are these two huge pictures of you at a restaurant holding hands over the table and smiling at each other. It's pretty unmistakable that you're more than friends."

That was more or less what they'd been warned to expect, but something in him must have been hoping, because the disappointment was intense. Lucien slumped in his chair and met Simon's gaze, seeing the same feeling reflected there.

A loud sound came through the phone, and Simon furrowed his brow.

"Ben, was that a truck?" he asked. "Where are you?"

Léo chuckled. "We are still at the tobacconist. Ben is experiencing a moral dilemma. He does not wish to support the newspaper by purchasing a copy, but since he has now read the article, he feels that to not purchase would be stealing."

Ben squawked a protest as Lucien and Simon grinned at each other, momentarily distracted. "It's not a 'moral dilemma.' You don't need to make it sound stupid. It's a… a… fuck. Fine, it's a moral dilemma."

Simon was still smiling as he said, "Give your conscience a break, Ben, and buy the paper. We need you to take pics and send them to us—there's no way either of us is going out to get one, and I don't think we're willing to subscribe online and give them our credit card details."

"Oh—good point," Ben said, and a moment later Léo added, "He's gone to buy it. Thank you, Simon. I was very much afraid that we'd be here all morning."

"Thank *you*," Simon replied sincerely. "If it weren't for your contacts, Luc and I would be hungry and unguarded right now. And have no idea what that damn article actually said."

"Luc?" Léo asked, a note of disbelief in his voice, and Lucien groaned. Simon winced and shot him an apologetic look. "You call him Luc? Nobody's ever called him anything except Lucien."

"It's a pet name," Lucien defended, wondering why he bothered.

"Oh, I know," Léo said, laughing. "Luc."

"No. Absolutely not." It was a losing battle.

"Ben's coming back. We'll go home and send you some pictures. Talk to you soon, *Luc*."

"Did you just call Lucien Luc?" Lucien heard Ben ask right before the call was disconnected. He stared at the phone in his hand.

"Sorry?" Simon said tentatively. Lucien looked up at him. "It just slipped out."

Lucien began to laugh.

IN the end, that Sunday was spent mostly in bed. They'd tried watching TV to keep busy, but the constant "news" updates about their relationship quickly became tiresome. It was enough that they were in touch with Guy every hour or so as he worked with various media outlets to show their relationship in a positive, nonscandalous light. There were many more demands for interviews than they'd anticipated, and he and Simon had agreed to discuss the possibility of doing one or two.

Lucien was fairly certain he knew how that discussion would go.

Early on Monday morning, with the help of the two security guards they'd hired plus four of their colleagues, Lucien and Simon left the apartment and headed for the executive airport. They'd considered just having a helicopter pick them up, but the roof of the building wasn't suitable, and as Simon said, if they had to leave the building to get to a helipad, they may as well just go to the airport.

Running the gauntlet of the press wasn't as bad as it could have been. For one thing, the property's Grand Canal location meant there wasn't a lot of space for people to gather in front of the building, and every time too many boats had gathered, the police came along to disperse them, as it affected traffic. There were the usual shouted questions, flashing cameras, and then, when it appeared Lucien and Simon weren't going to comment, some attempts to goad them with insults. Within a few minutes, they were safely aboard the private boat the security service had arranged, and headed to a private dock where they could transfer to a car.

When they finally reached the airport, a Morel plane was waiting to take Simon to Budapest. Another was coming for Lucien but had to take members of the executive team to a meeting in Prague first—he had reserved one of the airport's meeting rooms to work in while he waited. He walked with Simon to the gate.

"You'll be back in Paris on Wednesday, yes?" he asked, thinking that two days suddenly seemed like a lifetime.

"Yes," Simon said. "And I'm there for the rest of the week. I suppose I should look at some more apartments." The lack of enthusiasm in his voice was distinct, and an impulse hit Lucien so strongly, he could not ignore it.

"Don't. Stay with me."

Simon blinked at him. "What? You mean… move in with you?"

"Well, there wouldn't be a lot of moving in to do," Lucien said with a smirk. "Most of your things are there already—you'd just need whatever else you want from London."

"Be serious, Luc. You want me to live with you?" There was something achingly vulnerable about the look on Simon's face right then, and Lucien both loved and hated it. Loved that he could make Simon feel so deeply, and hated that Simon, his strong, amazing hero, should ever feel unsure about anything.

"Yes. *Yes.* I want you to live with me. I love you. This is not a casual relationship, Simon. We would end up living together eventually anyway—why must we be apart just for the sake of a foolish convention that says it is too soon?"

Simon's face lit up in a smile, and he leaned forward and kissed Lucien. As always when their lips touched, Lucien felt warm tingles flood up through his body. Kissing Simon was the most addictive thing on the planet.

"Yes," Simon said when they finally pulled apart. "Okay, yes. I want to live with you." They kissed again, until one of the airport officials discreetly cleared her throat. Lucien let Simon go and glanced at her, and then at the door.

"Are they waiting?" he asked, and she nodded.

"I'm sorry, sir, but you'll lose the slot."

"Thank you," Simon told her. "I can't miss this meeting." He grabbed his bag, squeezed Lucien's hand, and then turned for the gate. "I'll call you tonight."

Chapter Thirteen

SIMON leaned against the headboard in another nice but anonymous hotel and waited for Lucien to answer the phone. He was bone tired. The weekend, which had started so perfectly, had ended up being a complete energy suck.

"Hello." Lucien's warm voice in his ear was better than twelve hours' sleep. Si felt muscles relax that he hadn't even realized were tense.

"Hi," he said on a long sigh. "How was your day?" He chuckled. Who'd have thought he'd ever be so domestic?

"Not terrible, considering," Lucien replied. "There was press in front of the apartment and the corporate building, but I have not had to deal with them directly yet. And your day?"

Si slumped down in the bed. "I'm chalking it up as a success. I got a few odd looks, one person congratulated me, and a few sympathized over the intrusion of the media—which I thought was pretty good of them, since it must have been a pain in the arse for them to have the press outside their building—but the meeting itself went well, and there was a lot of support for On the Ball."

Lucien sighed quietly, and Si heard the relief in it. "So, it's going to be okay."

"Yeah, I think so. I mean, I don't know how that Italian guy from Friday would have acted if I'd met with him today, to be honest, but overall I think it shouldn't be too bad. I spoke with Anna before, and Tim, and they said there's been a lot of curiosity, lots of calls from the press, but we're still getting as many, if not more applications—and the training camp is now officially full." He paused. Anna had also told him that several applications had been withdrawn. That made him sad, but more so that people in need were unwilling to accept help simply because they didn't approve of the person offering it.

"What about the withdrawals?" Lucien asked gently, and Si smiled.

"You've been talking to Anna, too."

"I stopped at the office on my way from the airport," he acknowledged. "I wanted to make sure they didn't need anything. We have a security guard on the door for the next few days."

Si frowned, not liking that. Of course he didn't want Anna and Michel subjected to the press, but…. "Won't that discourage anybody stopping by to ask about the program?"

"Possibly, but the guard has been instructed to be as polite as possible. The offices don't get many visitors anyway." Lucien's tone was firm. "We need to make sure our staff and visitors are protected."

If it were possible for hearts to melt, Si thought his might just have done so. How could he ever have considered Lucien just another billionaire businessman? He cared so much about his people—and about Simon.

"Okay," he acquiesced. "You're right. And if it's only for a few days, it doesn't really matter anyway."

"It wasn't negotiable," Lucien said dryly, and Si wasn't sure whether to chuckle or let the stab of annoyance take over. There was his autocratic billionaire.

"My mum rang me today," he said, in a bid to change the subject. From Lucien's sharply indrawn breath, Si guessed he'd just realized they hadn't given a thought to warning Si's family.

"We should have called your parents as soon as we found out." The regret in Lucien's voice was clear. "This is not a good start to my relationship with them."

The laugh burst from Si before he could stop it. "I guess not. I think they'll forgive you, though. Mum thinks you're 'awfully fit.'"

There was a pause, and Si could almost hear Lucien thinking about that. "Is that good?" he asked finally, and Si laughed again.

"Yes. But if she giggles and blushes when you meet her, ignore it."

"When will that be, do you think?"

Si felt that warm, melty sensation again. He'd never brought anyone home to his parents before. "Soon," he said through a suddenly tight throat. "Maybe next time I have a meeting in the UK, you can come?"

"I'll tell Paul to call Anna and check your schedule." There was a slight tremor in Lucien's voice.

Was he nervous about meeting Si's family? That was so sweet.

They talked for a little longer about nothing important. It was so comforting to hear Lucien's voice that Si didn't want to end the call, even though he was tired and knew Lucien must be too. Finally they said good night, and Si went to bed in his impersonal hotel room secure in the knowledge that everything was going to be okay.

HIS phone woke him at a little before six. Groaning, he squinted at the screen.

"Lucien? What's wrong?" He wasn't awake enough to feel anything other than grumpy, but he knew such an early call couldn't be good.

"One of the Italian papers is making some nasty allegations," Lucien said tersely. "I'm sending you a link. Guy thinks we need to give an interview as soon as possible."

Si sat up, blinking away the last of his sleep as his phone buzzed with an incoming message. "What allegations?" he asked. Damn it, things had been *good*. Why did life have to step in and screw with them?

"Read the article. I have to make some calls, but I'll call you back in fifteen minutes." The line went dead, and Simon opened Lucien's message with his stomach in knots. What did it take to make his scrupulously polite lover hang up without saying goodbye?

Fuck.

He skimmed the translated article, bile rising in his throat. *Not good*. It was all groundless conjecture, but of the kind that could cause maximum harm to On the Ball. Supposition that Édouard Morel had basically bought him for Lucien, who—according to "sources close to Lucien Morel"—had always had a crush on him. Well, that was true, but the idea that Lucien would need to pay for sex was laughable.

It got worse.

Aside from earning the money for the program on his back—because apparently ongoing funding for On the Ball was contingent on him "servicing" Lucien—there were also some shady suggestions that participants in the program would be required to provide similar services to earn their funding.

His phone rang, and he answered it automatically. "Simon?"

"So basically I'm both a whore and a pimp to teenagers," he said faintly.

Lucien sighed. "Nobody with any sense believes that," he answered firmly. "And my father is stepping in since the article impugns both him and the Morel Corporation."

"How many people are lacking in sense?" Si asked. He knew how the media worked. Sensationalism was everything, even if there wasn't an iota of truth in a story.

Lucien's hesitation spoke volumes, and Si's brain clicked into gear. "The morning shows," he said, and scrambled for the remote control.

"Simon, don't—" Lucien began, but Si had already turned on the TV. The hotel had a good assortment of news channels in several languages, and they all seemed to be reporting on the same thing, if the clips of him and Lucien were any indication. He'd never wished more that he spoke multiple languages.

"Sum it up for me, Lucien. How bad is it? Be honest."

"It's bad," Lucien said bluntly. "But it's not terrible. Many of the news outlets are calling the article unfounded, without evidence. The morning show presenters are wondering where the information comes from—and people are calling in. There is a lot of nastiness, but also a lot of support. It's still early, but I don't think this is the end." He hesitated again. "To be honest, I think if they'd stopped at just saying you prostituted yourself for the money, things might be worse. But bringing the kids into it has got everyone up in arms, and they're questioning the validity of the entire article. Which is good."

"Yeah," Si said, his gaze glued to the TV, where two presenters were shaking their heads as they discussed something—in Spanish?—one of the infamous hand-holding pictures in the background. This was not good, no matter what Lucien said. "So what now? Did you say Guy wants us to do an interview?"

"Yes, but first my father is going to release a statement. Guy is carefully thinking about the best options for our interview. In the meantime, business as usual, and don't talk to the press."

"Because I was planning an intimate lunch with the paparazzi," Si snarked, hugging his pillow as he surfed slowly through the channels, seeing more of the same.

Lucien sighed. "I know you weren't, but you know they'll be desperate for something they can use. Don't let them goad you, no matter how horrible they are."

"I won't," Si muttered sulkily. He knew he was being a wanker, but he couldn't seem to help it. Christ, it wasn't every day a man was called a whore and a pimp.

He heard Lucien sigh again and felt a pang of guilt. This wasn't Lucien's fault—in fact, Lucien was only in this train wreck because of Si.

"I'll speak to you later," Lucien said, and the word tore from Si before he knew he was speaking.

"Luc!"

Pause. "Yes, Simon?"

"I'm sorry. I'm sorry I'm being such a tosser. I'll get over it, I promise. I love you." Si could hear the faintly pleading tone to his own voice.

"I love you, Simon. Even when you are being a 'tosser.'"

Si snorted a laugh, feeling better. Things were still shit, but Lucien loved him.

THINGS were shit, and nothing could make them better.

Si sat on the edge of the hotel bed, staring at his phone with loathing. It was stupid, because it wasn't the phone's fault that everything was going so badly—no, so *catastrophically*—but it seemed to Si that every time he answered the damn phone, it all got worse.

He'd been just about to leave for his first meeting when the bloody thing had rung. It had been the youth club he was meeting with—and they'd canceled. They hadn't said it was because he was a pimp whore—or should that be whore pimp?—but their hastily mumbled excuses were pretty transparent, especially when they hadn't been interested in rescheduling.

No sooner had he hung up than the next call had come, from his appointment for the afternoon—canceling. They'd been more honest than the youth club, outright saying that they were unwilling to be associated with any negative publicity. They did invite him to call them again if the bad press settled down. Si had bitten his tongue to keep from telling them "thanks for nothing."

Now he glared at his phone, feeling like an idiot for wanting to smash the damn thing into a million pieces, bury them, and have the "grave" concreted over. He hated that he was in Budapest for no reason, that if he tried to take a commercial flight home—back to Paris, where he could hide in Lucien's apartment and be cuddled and comforted by the best man in the world—he would be mobbed by the paparazzi as soon as he got to the airport. He hated that he needed to call Lucien and ask for the use of a Morel plane, and he hated that Lucien would know what that meant—that things weren't okay after all.

He hated that because of small-minded pettiness and hateful rumormongering, he was denied the joy of basking in his and Lucien's newfound love.

It wasn't fair.

He'd always been good to the press. During his playing days, he'd never turned down an interview. Never denied them a sound bite after a match, no matter how exhausted or disappointed he was. Same with the public—he'd participated in more fan events and fundraisers than he could count, agreeing to every one the club's PR department had suggested. He'd signed autographs when he was out with friends and family, never refusing even when fans interrupted meals or accosted him in airport lounges.

Yet now that he finally got a chance to realize his dream, to help kids fulfill their dreams, now that he'd finally fallen in love and wanted to be happy... people were shitting all over it. Why? To sell fucking tabloids.

Life sucked.

Sighing, he lifted his phone, but he just couldn't do it. He couldn't bring himself to call Lucien and tell him exactly how bad things were. He couldn't bring himself to call Anna and find out that his program was collapsing around his ears.

He just couldn't.

He swiped the screen, tapped on a contact, and lifted the phone to his ear.

"Bonjour, Simon," Paul's silky voice said. "Aren't you supposed to be on your way to a meeting? Is something wrong?"

It didn't surprise Si in the least that Paul knew where he was supposed to be. Not only had he and Anna bonded, but Paul was the master of Lucien's schedule, and how could he ensure Lucien's happiness if he didn't know where Lucien's lover was?

"I need a favor, Paul," he said tersely, then stopped and took a deep breath. "I'm sorry. It's been a... rough morning." He glanced at the clock beside the bed and grimaced. It wasn't even nine o'clock yet. "Can you please arrange for me to get back to Paris as soon as possible?"

Paul didn't even hesitate, although Si knew he had to have questions. "Of course. I'll call you back in five minutes with the arrangements."

Relief flooded through Si. *Yes.* He could go home to Lucien, lock the apartment door, and just forget about the world for a little while. "Thank you. Um... could you not tell Lucien? I-I want to... surprise him." Wow, that was a poor effort. If Paul hadn't known before that something was up, he did now.

The long pause said more clearly than any words could that Paul was fully aware of the situation. "I think perhaps Lucien will not be as surprised as you expect," he said finally, and Si shut his eyes. What the hell was happening? Should he turn on the TV or check the news headlines?

"Paul, I don't want to pile anything else on his shoulders until I'm there and can tell him not to worry to his face," he confessed. "You know him. You know how deeply he feels things, even if he pretends not to. Please, just get me back there, and I'll tell him everything, but I don't want him worrying more than he already is."

"I will call you back in five minutes," Paul promised. Si took that as agreement and murmured his thanks.

While he waited, he packed up the few things he had with him, and checked the weather forecast, forcing himself not to look at any news or gossip sites. It was a little over six minutes later—not that he was keeping track—when the phone rang in his hand. Even though he was expecting the call, knew what it was about, his hand trembled a little as he answered.

"Hello?"

"Simon, it's Paul." He knew that, of course, and Paul knew he knew—the joys of caller ID—but it was oddly reassuring to be told.

"Hi. Please tell me you have good news."

"I do. None of the Morel planes are available until late this afternoon, but I spoke with Léo, and he's sending the Artois family plane for you. It will be there in a little less than three hours. I called the executive airport and reserved a meeting room for you with butler service. If you want to leave the hotel, you can wait there, and they'll make sure you have everything you need."

Yes. Si wanted out of this hotel. "I'm heading there now." After the debacle of Sunday, Lucien had insisted he have a security guard and private car at his disposal, so all he had to do was text the driver that he needed to leave.

"I will clear Lucien's schedule for the late afternoon," Paul told him, and Si was assailed by guilt.

"I don't want to put anyone out," he began, but Paul interrupted.

"It is just a budget meeting, and not one he really needs to go to. They just like to have him there to lend them importance."

"If you're sure," Si said, both amused by Paul's perspective and desperately longing for Lucien to be free when he got back to Paris.

"I am positive. Make certain you take advantage of the butler service. Have you had breakfast? Lucien will be very cross if you come home faint from hunger."

Si was laughing as he ended the call.

HE should have stayed in the hotel room. At least there, nobody had looked at him with curiosity—or accusation. He hadn't had to face the stares of a thousand questions. No one at the executive airport had dared to ask or comment, but behind their scrupulous politeness he could sense tumultuous opinion.

Even holed up in the private meeting room, he didn't feel secure. The butler had been impeccably professional, and he'd had food and coffee, but… was he imagining it? It felt like every time someone glanced at him, they were thinking of that article. *Whore. Pimp.*

By the time the butler came to tell him the plane had arrived and was ready for him, Si was on the verge of jumping out of his skin. He followed the man to the correct gate, wishing he'd *walk faster, dammit*, and then waited impatiently as the airport official checked his ID before escorting him onto the tarmac.

Nearly there.

He scaled the steps to the plane, counting each one that brought him closer to Paris. Just a few more hours. He just had to make it through a few more hours, and he would be with people who cared about him, who didn't judge or believe horrible stories. Just a few more hours.

He crossed through the doorway—and stopped.

"I have a message from Paul," Léo said. "He understands your wish not to worry Lucien, but believes that you should worry about yourself also. And he thinks you should lean on your friends. So we are here for you to lean on."

Si dropped his bag and let Léo, Ben, and Malik crowd him into a group hug.

THE plane took off smoothly, and Si leaned back in his seat. It was so nice not to be alone.

Beside him, Ben chattered about something or other, Léo smiling indulgently at him while Malik rolled his eyes, but he was smiling, too.

"As glad as I am to see you all," Si said, "why are you here?"

Ben shrugged. "Paul called Léo to ask if you could borrow a plane, since the Morel ones were all tied up. Léo's sister-in-law had actually brought the plane down to Nice for the day, to visit a friend or go shopping or something—I'm not sure exactly—so Léo said no problem, and then Paul said since the plane was going to be leaving from Nice, would we mind going with it, because he thought you might need some friends."

"Thank you," Si told them sincerely. "You have no idea how much I needed friends. I-I should have called Luc, but he's convinced himself this is all going to work out okay, and I wanted him to have just a few more hours of that."

"What happened?" Léo asked, just as Malik said,

"Luc? Seriously? We're calling him Luc now? Since when?"

"I'm calling him Luc," Si said. "You and everyone else are calling him Lucien."

Malik snorted, a gleeful grin spreading across his face, and Si ignored it to answer Léo.

"The two appointments I had lined up for the day canceled. One was blunt enough to say it was because of the article. I'm scared to ring Anna and find out what else is happening."

Malik whipped out his phone. "I'll do it. What's the number?"

Si hesitated. He really did need to know what was going on... but....

"Malik, put that away. Simon will call when he's ready," Ben chastised, and Si smiled gratefully at him. Still....

"No, I need to know." He reached for his phone, glad that being on a private plane meant he could use it, then paused. "It's easier with you all here. Thank you."

Ben squeezed his arm, and a few moments later he was listening to the phone ring in his ear. And ring. And ri—

"On the Ball, this is Tim."

Si's chest squeezed.

"Tim," he managed to choke out, but that was all he needed.

"Si? Mate, is that you?" Tim's tone changed from slightly brusque to concerned.

"Yes."

"Why haven't you been answering my texts? I didn't want to call because I figured you were getting tons of those, but I wanted to make sure you were okay."

Si blinked. "I—I didn't get any texts from you. Wait, let me check." He pulled the phone away from his ear and navigated to his texting app. Sure enough, there were a half-dozen texts from Tim. Why hadn't the phone chimed, or left a notification on the screen? He put the phone back to his ear. "I did get them, but I didn't see them. I'm sorry."

Tim blew out a breath. "No worries, as long as you're all right."

Making a face even though Tim couldn't see him, Si said, "It hasn't been the best day of my life."

"No kidding? Mate, just remember that nobody who knows you would ever believe that tripe. This is going to blow over."

A lump formed in Si's throat. "Yeah, that might be wishful thinking, Tim. I'm on a plane on my way back to Paris. My meetings for today both canceled."

"I guessed as much," Tim replied, surprising Si. "Why do you think I'm in the office? My appointments canceled too. But Si, it's only a temporary setback."

"Right." Si couldn't bear to argue the point. Tim had invested so much hope in this program—it was supposed to be a second chance for him, a new beginning.

Time for a subject change. "Uh, why didn't Anna answer the phone?"

Was Tim hesitating? "Anna's run off her feet, mate. The phone's been ringing off the hook."

That couldn't be good. "The press?" he asked.

Another hesitation. "Yeah, partly."

Fuck. "How many more appointments were canceled?" he asked. "How many—" Fuck, he was afraid to ask. "How many applications have been withdrawn?"

Tim's silence spoke volumes.

"Right. Well… I guess that's it."

"No!" Tim's shout was so loud that Si pulled the phone away from his ear. "No, Si. That's not it. People are nervous because they don't know what's going on. Yes, there were a lot of meeting cancellations, but there have only been a few applications withdrawn, and only *three* kids pulled out of the training camp. Only three, and those kids are *paying* to attend. There's a lot of support for you and the program online, Si. Once Mr. Morel gives his statement, and you and Lucien do the interview, things will turn around. In the meantime, you still have a lot of kids relying on you and this program. Don't give up."

Si pressed the heel of his hand against his eye. Tim was right. Things looked bad, but he hadn't done anything wrong, and after working for so long toward this goal, he'd be a moron to give up now. "Right," he said. "I'll be back in a few hours. Let me know if anything urgent comes up, but otherwise we'll plan to have a full staff meeting first thing tomorrow morning. Tell Anna and Michel?"

"I'll tell them," Tim promised. "Si, I know you're worried. And you've copped the worst of this. But I really think this is going to pass."

"Thank you," Si said. He wasn't convinced, but what was the point in saying so? One of them would be proved right, and he sincerely hoped it wasn't him.

THEY finally landed in Paris. Paul had a car waiting for them that whisked them to Lucien's apartment, where they set up camp in front of the TV—although Malik and Léo firmly refused to let him watch any of the news or gossip channels. Instead, they found a suitably awful movie on Netflix, and spent an hour picking it apart. If he hadn't been so preoccupied, he would have had fun. He'd tried telling his babysitters that he would be fine on his own if they needed to get back to Monaco, but Ben had just given him a don't-bullshit-me look, and said they'd been meaning to check in on Léo's Paris apartment, anyway.

It gave Si a warm feeling.

By the time he heard Lucien's key in the door, he'd managed to block out most of the drama of the last few days. Lucien's imminent arrival brought it all flooding back—but that was a small price to pay for having him there. Si scrambled off the couch, and as a surprised-looking Lucien appeared in the doorway, he threw himself into his arms and buried his face in the crook of Lucien's neck.

"Simon?" The concern in Lucien's voice was pretty much his undoing. He wrapped his arms around Lucien's waist and squeezed. Lucien squeezed back, and something settled inside Si.

They could ride this out. It would be tough, but it could be done.

Taking a deep breath, he stepped back. "Surprise?" He forced himself to smile and met Lucien's gaze.

Lucien raised a perfect blond eyebrow. "It is a surprise. No wonder Paul insisted I come right home. And you brought people—beggars you found in Budapest?" he teased, even as he circled an arm around Si's waist and pulled him close.

"Ha ha," Malik said. "You're so funny—Luc."

Si bit the inside of his cheek as Lucien's grip tightened suddenly, and hurried to intervene. "Léo was kind enough to lend me a plane to get home when my meetings were canceled," he explained. "And they were at loose ends today, so they decided to come along."

Lucien leaned over and kissed his cheek. "Your meetings were canceled?" he asked, and Si swallowed. It still caused a burn in his stomach.

"You haven't spoken to Anna today, have you?" he deflected.

"No." Lucien tugged him over to their favorite armchair, sat, and pulled Si down on his lap. They were both big enough that it wasn't entirely comfortable, but Si was willing to sacrifice comfort to be this close to his lover. "What happened?"

"You know what happened." With a sigh, Si rested his head beside Lucien's on the high back of the chair. "That damn article freaked people out. Every appointment I had for this week has been canceled— same with Tim. And about half of next week's have, too. I figure the rest are just waiting to see what happens next before they decide."

"When is your father's press conference, Lucien?" Léo asked from the couch. Si turned his head to look.

"In about half an hour," Lucien replied, and Si snapped his head back so fast his neck cracked.

"What? It's today?"

"Yes. It would actually have been earlier, but Guy thought this might be better—sound bites for the evening news. They banned me from being there, though, because they didn't want any distractions."

"We can watch it here, then," Ben said, reaching for his phone.

"Don't wake Dani," Léo told him, and Ben pouted.

"I have to," he declared. "She was on Twitter for hours today—well, last night, her time—keeping track of everything for us. She deserves to see the press conference live."

"She deserves to get a good night's sleep before she has to go to work," Léo countered. Si was caught between amusement, and being freaked out that a woman he didn't know had apparently been keeping track of the disaster his life had become. Ben had mentioned Dani several times, but she was still a stranger.

Ben leaped to his feet and planted his hand on his hips. "Whose BFF is she?" he demanded. "Mine! I think I know what she'd want, and I'm telling you, if she finds out I could have woken her for this and didn't, there will be hell to pay."

Lucien made a choked sound and turned his head to hide his face against Si's neck. Léo shrugged, and Ben, a victorious expression on his face, tapped the screen of his phone and lifted it to his ear.

"I'm sorry, I'm sorry!" he exclaimed almost immediately. "But I thought you'd want to know that Lucien's dad is giving the press conference in about twenty-five minutes." He shot Léo a smug look. "Yeah, I figured. Léo didn't want me to wake you—whoa! I did, though, so it's all good."

Malik was outright laughing, but Si and Lucien managed to restrain themselves to a few smothered chuckles.

"Sure, call me back," Ben said. "Talk soon." He ended the call and looked at his boyfriend. "She's going to make coffee and stuff and then we'll watch it together."

Léo just smiled. "I am sorry I questioned you," he said, and Ben grinned. He turned to look at Si and Lucien.

"Dani has put together a petition—well, I'm not sure if it's actually a petition, since it's not petitioning anyone. A survey? I don't know."

"What kind of petition—or survey?" Lucien asked patiently.

"Let me show you." Ben came over and perched on the arm of the chair, making an already crowded situation even worse. He tapped at his phone, then turned the screen to face them.

Si swallowed hard.

It was an online petition site, with a petition—or survey, or whatever—open. The title was "Show Your Support for Simon Wood, Lucien Morel, and On the Ball Soccer Charity."

It had 351,974 signatures. As he watched, the number jumped to 351,979, and then again to 351,986.

"When... when did she set this up?" Was that his voice? It was so shaky.

"Right after the article came out this morning, so, what... about ten hours ago? She actually called before Lucien did, and she was so pissed. Dani's kind of a crusader sometimes, and it really bugs her that you're doing something worthwhile and these buzzards are trying to ruin it. She left work early and was on social media all afternoon and evening."

Si bit his lip hard. Beneath him, Lucien was breathing unsteadily.

"That's... very kind of her." What the hell could he say? He never would have expected a stranger to go to such lengths on his behalf. He'd have to talk to Lucien later about sending her something to show the depth of their appreciation. *Like what? Diamonds?*

"I think you should read some of the messages people left," Ben told them. "I'm going to send you a link, but here... have a look while I go get some water." He thrust the phone into Lucien's hand, and then wandered off toward the kitchen. Si cleared his throat and leaned closer to Lucien, his eyes glued to the small screen. Lucien lifted a trembling hand and tapped the comments section.

Simon and Lucien should be commended for the work they're doing, not harassed!

Simon + Lucien 4eva

On the Ball will help kids fulfill dreams. So sad that some people are trying to ruin it.

You guys are awesome, keep up the good work :-)

Dipshits will always be dipshits, but we all know good people when we see them, and Lucien Morel and Simon Wood are good people.

Play sports. Love each other. Ignore everything else.

Don't let the h8ters get you down.

You guys are so cute together! Everyone deserves a love like that.

The truth will out, Simon and Lucien. Be strong.

*I'm sorry this is happening to you. *hugs**

It went on, thousands of comments, congratulating them on their relationship, lauding their efforts with On the Ball, and unfailingly offering support. Si choked on a sob, and only then realized he was crying. He swiped at his eyes and looked at Lucien, who was biting his lip so hard it was bleeding.

"Luc," he said, and grabbed a tissue from the box on the side table. "Here." He stroked Lucien's cheek until his jaw relaxed, and then dabbed at the cut.

"Did you *bite your lip*?" Malik asked, shock reverberating through his voice. Si paused, glanced over his shoulder, and was shocked himself by the expressions on Malik's and Léo's faces. It was just a bitten lip, but from the look of them, Lucien may as well have spit on the carpet.

"What?" he asked. Lucien took the tissue from him, and Si stood, scrubbing at his face again. His skin felt itchy with the drying tears. "It's not a bad bite. It won't need stitches or anything."

"What won't need stitches?" Ben asked, coming back in holding a bottle of the fancy water Lucien's housekeeper kept the fridge stocked with.

"Lucien bit his lip," Si told him, "and those two are acting like the Pope groped a ninety-year-old nun."

Ben snorted. "For them, that might be less shocking. The school they were at gave out detentions for things like lip biting or running hands through hair. And I don't know what Lucien's nanny was like, but Léo's used to punish him for it, too."

Si blinked, and looked at Lucien. "Really?"

The lip had stopped bleeding, and Lucien nodded solemnly. "Nervous tics and habits are a detraction. One should appear poised at all times."

What the hell? Si didn't know what to say to that. He'd noticed how calm and unruffled Lucien always was, of course, but he'd just put that down to personality. Was it really forced repression?

"So there are times when you want to, I don't know, bite your lip or rub your forehead or something, and you have to force yourself not to feel?"

In a single smooth motion, Lucien was out of the chair and standing before him. He dropped a kiss on Si's mouth. "I never force myself not to feel. I force myself not to fidget. When I was a child, it was very difficult, but over time I have found it beneficial. Now when I have the urge to bite my lip or rub my forehead, I ask myself why I feel this way, and instead attempt to deal with whatever is causing me to feel unbalanced.

It rarely fails—only when I am feeling too much." He tapped his lip, smiling ruefully.

That kind of made sense, although Si still felt there was something wrong with it.

"Are we going to watch the press conference?" Ben asked, turning on the television. Si took advantage of Lucien's momentary distraction to steal his chair. Lucien protested as Ben called Dani in the background, and they were still bickering about it minutes later when Malik warned, "It's starting."

Lucien planted himself on the arm of the chair, and they all turned their attention to the screen. Édouard Morel was sitting at a table in a hotel function room, Guy on one side and a women Lucien identified as the head of the corporation's legal team on the other. The room was filled with members of the press.

Édouard spoke—in French.

"What's he saying?" Si asked urgently.

"Shit," Ben said. "I didn't think of that. Dani, what channel are you watching?"

"Sky News," a clear feminine voice answered, startling Si, who hadn't realized Ben had the phone on loudspeaker. Léo grabbed the remote control from Ben and flipped quickly through the satellite channels until he found the right one.

"… deeply concerned about allegations made in the press that smear the reputation of my company, of my family, and of myself. The Morel Corporation has been a backbone of the French and European economies for generations. We have constantly and consistently supported the growth of industry, the development of new technology, and made considerable charitable contributions for the betterment of society. It is disturbing and hurtful to realize that despite all this, certain members of the press feel no compunction about making harmful and completely false accusations about us as we endeavor to assist young people in achieving their dreams." Édouard paused for a beat, his face solemn. "The idea that I, acting in my position as head of the Morel Corporation, used company funds to buy sex for my son; that my son would indeed accept any such action without demanding my immediate resignation and full restitution of said funds to the company; that Simon Wood, an upstanding and admirable man, would prostitute himself; and that the Morel Corporation, my son and I, and Mr. Wood would ever conspire to prostitute children, is not only completely false and absurd, it is also defamatory, and we will be filing legal suit against the *newspaper*"—his mouth twisted slightly in a sneer—"and their parent company."

Several reporters began to shout questions, but Édouard held up a hand.

"When Simon Wood approached me with his plan to form a charity to provide financial aid to children to play football, I was hesitant. Many who know me know that I have never before given funds to sports charities. My belief was always that charity was for necessities: food, shelter, health, and education. This is something my son, Lucien, has argued about with me often over the years. Lucien believes that by feeding the soul we are able to improve the state of the body. Simon's passion and enthusiasm for his program reminded me of Lucien's arguments, and I wondered if perhaps I was too set in my ways, if I was overlooking an important element of the human experience. I have a great deal of respect for my son as a person and as a businessman, and although then I did not know him personally, Simon has shown himself over the years to be dedicated, hardworking, and a role model for young people. If two men worthy of such respect both espoused the same idea, perhaps I needed to open myself to the possibility. It was for this reason that I agreed to provide funding for On the Ball.

"However, my reason for volunteering Lucien as a business consultant was threefold. I honestly believed he could provide necessary assistance for the program without costing any of the funds designated for charitable use. In addition to this, I knew he would enjoy this task, enjoy being able to work on a project he had long been trying to convince me to take on. But perhaps most importantly in my eyes, I believed that Lucien and Simon would be well-suited to each other—"

Lucien leaped to his feet, Si gasped, and the press roared.

"What is he *doing*?" Dani squealed through the phone. Malik just shook his head, while Léo snatched up his own phone, then just stared at it helplessly.

Only Ben was calm. "Shh," he said. "Wait and see what he says next."

As Édouard waited silently, the members of the press slowly quietened.

"As I was saying, I believed the qualities I saw in Simon Wood that day—passion, intelligence, determination, and drive—added to what I knew of him in his professional guise, made him an excellent match for my son. Like many parents, I want my son to be happy. I want him to find love. I have, over the years, introduced him to many people I felt may make good prospective partners for him. I would not have spent millions of dollars to act as matchmaker, but since I had already made the decision to allocate that money to the charity, I saw no problem with ensuring Lucien and Simon would have an opportunity to meet and get to know each other—without knowing that I was being an interfering old goat." He stopped, and after a moment of stunned silence, the shouted questions began.

Chaos reigned, and Si took advantage of the moment to suck in a much-needed deep breath. As an assistant called for the press to settle down and selected the first reporter to ask a question, Si grabbed Lucien's hand and tugged him back down to sit on the arm of the chair.

"Did you know?" he murmured, although from the shell-shocked expression on his lover's face, he didn't need to ask. Lucien shook his head.

"Mr. Morel, if the charity hadn't been worthy of having funds allocated, what would you have done?"

"Not allocated them," Édouard said promptly. "And then spoken to my wife and had her find another way for Lucien to meet Simon."

Malik chuckled. "You two didn't have a chance," he heckled.

"Monsieur Morel, you maintain that On the Ball is a completely legitimate charity, and that none of the beneficiaries would be required to earn funding in any way?"

"That is correct. We invite anyone who believes otherwise to present their evidence. In fact, in an attempt to show our complete transparency, we have decided to have the program investigated and assessed." He named an independent consulting firm that specialized in reviewing companies under legal question. Their reputation was above reproach—as were their prices. Si winced.

"Who's paying for that?" he muttered. Lucien hushed him.

"Mr. Morel, you mentioned having introduced your son to many prospective partners over the years. Did you mean both men and women?"

The room fell silent, and many reporters turned incredulous gazes on the speaker while others kept their eyes glued to Édouard, faces alight with the hope of a juicy sound bite.

Édouard leaned forward so the microphone would catch his every word. "I have known since Lucien was a teenager that he was bisexual. He came to his mother and me when he was fifteen and told us. He had prepared a presentation, which included referenced information on exactly what it meant to be bisexual, some of the misconceptions around it, and resources to help parents and families of bisexual people understand and be supportive. As I sat there and listened for forty-five minutes, I saw in my son honesty, integrity, intelligence, and attention to detail. These are traits my wife and I passed on to him both genetically and by instilling them in him during his formative years. He's our son. We love him. And we don't care if he loves a man or a woman, as long as he's happy."

Lucien made a choked sound and fled to the kitchen. Si followed as Édouard took another question.

"Hey." He laid a hand on Lucien's back where he stood with his fists propped against the counter. Lucien turned and wrapped his arms around him, burying his face against Si's neck. It was wet with tears.

Si held him, and they just stood there, breathing together. Eventually, Lucien inhaled a shuddering breath and stepped back.

"I have never cried so much in my life as I have today," he declared, scrubbing his hands over his face.

Si grinned. "Me either," he admitted. "But how brilliant is it that we're crying because people love us and want to show support?"

Lucien turned on the tap and stuck his wrists under the faucet. "It is amazing," he agreed. "My father.... My parents have always supported me. Even that day, when I told them and I was so nervous, they were unfailingly supportive. They told me they loved me no matter what. But...."

"But you've never been in a position where they might have to prove that? Until now."

Turning off the tap, Lucien reached for a dishcloth. "Exactly. It is... so reassuring to know that they are there for me." He met Si's gaze. "For us."

Smiling, Si took Lucien's hand. "It's going to be okay, isn't it?"

Lucien shrugged and squeezed his hand. "We'll have to wait and see."

The sound of a throat being cleared made them both turn to the doorway. "Sorry to interrupt," Ben said, "but are you guys all right?"

Si leaned against Lucien, loving the sensation of his body *right there*, his warmth, his smell. This was his, forever. "We're fine," he said. "It's been a tough week so far, but it's going to get better."

"You bet!" Dani's voice said, startling Si *yet again*. He'd seen the phone in Ben's hand, but it hadn't occurred to him that Dani would still be there. "Twitter's gone insane since the press conference started—don't worry, guys, by the time the internet is done, that paper will be out of business."

"Thank you, Dani, for everything you've done," Lucien told her, his body trembling slightly against Si's with the repressed amusement he could hear in his voice. "We can't begin to tell you how much it means."

"My pleasure," she replied, sounding utterly sincere. "I'm going to get a couple more hours' sleep before work, but keep me in the loop, yeah?"

"We will," Si promised, already thinking about what they could send her. He'd have to ask Ben what she liked.

Ben ended the call just as Malik came to the doorway. "Have we moved the party to the kitchen?"

Lucien snorted. "This isn't a party. People don't cry at *my* parties," he declared authoritatively, and Si laughed.

"Did you really give your parents a forty-five minute presentation on what it meant to be bisexual?" Malik asked, brow raised.

Shrugging, Lucien took Si's hand and led him back toward the living room. "Yes."

Malik shook his head. "You're the only person I know who could do that and make it seem cool."

A rush of affection swamped Si, and he tugged Lucien to a stop and kissed him. "That's because he is cool," he murmured, and warm blue eyes smiled back at him.

Chapter Fourteen

Two months later

LUCIEN walked into his kitchen and found his boyfriend sitting at the table in his underwear, head in his hands.

"What are you doing up?" he asked, although he knew. Simon had been worrying himself sick over the training camp for weeks, and it had only gotten worse over the last few days.

Looking up, Simon sighed. "Did I wake you? I'm sorry."

Lucien sat beside him and took his hand. "You know I don't sleep well when you're gone." And didn't that give him a little thrill? He'd slept alone most of his adult life, but after just a few months living with Simon, he didn't rest well without him by his side. "You need to let this go. Everything is going to be fine."

Simon smiled, but it was so obviously forced that Lucien raised a brow, and he stopped. "I know. I know everything is in place. I know there's no reason for anything to go wrong. I know I need a good night's sleep. But knowing all that doesn't make it any easier to accept."

They sat there in silence for a while, just holding hands. Finally Simon sighed again. "Okay. Let's go over the good things again. The training camp is completely full, has been for months, and there's a waiting list."

"Yes," Lucien affirmed.

"Applications for On the Ball's funding for this season exceeded our estimates by nearly 300 percent. We have a waiting list, and are desperately scrabbling for more money."

"Correct," Lucien said, and wondered if this was the time to tell his lover that he, Léo, Ben, and Malik were in the process of setting up a trust to fund a dozen applicants a year.

"We have a great team to run the training camp, and because of all the publicity, we were donated the use of a really good facility right outside Paris to run it from."

"Not to mention the positive media coverage over the last few weeks," Lucien added, and Simon nodded.

"Those scummy bastards at that Italian paper issued an apology and retraction when faced with the threat of legal action," he continued. "And support for us and On the Ball has been very high. Oh, I forgot to tell you—Dani texted me last week. We've apparently been 'shipped.'"

Lucien blinked. *Shipped?* His English had improved dramatically in just a few months, but that didn't make sense in any way. "Shipped?" he asked. "How…? Isn't that postage? How would we be shipped?"

Simon laughed, and watching his face light up made Lucien so happy that he resolved to make it happen more often.

"It's a pop-culture thing. When people are in a relation*ship*, their names get mixed together to form a relationship name. They're *shipped*."

Lucien considered that. It sounded stupid to him. Did people not have anything better to do? What was wrong with using both their names? "What is our ship name?" he asked.

"Simien."

That was just too much. "That's stupid," he pointed out, and Simon laughed again.

"I know! But it makes people happy, and a lot of those people have been donating to On the Ball. I promise you don't have to answer if anyone calls you that, though."

"Good." Because there was no way he ever would. It was bad enough that Malik and Léo sometimes called him Luc now—to tease, of course. Simon was the only one who called him that naturally. "But do you see all the good things?"

Simon stood, and tugged Lucien up with him. "Yeah. Come on, let's go back to bed. Morning will be here soon enough."

STANDING off to the side as Simon spoke with the camp's manager, Lucien struggled to restrain a smug grin. The weeklong camp had flown by with barely any problems, and those that had come up had been easily resolved. Simon had kept muttering about it being too good to be true, but now, just an hour before the camp would officially end, he finally seemed to be accepting its success.

"I'll be sorry to see this week end," a familiar voice said beside him, and Lucien turned to smile at Tim. Simon's friend had become a good friend to him, also, and when he was in Paris he often shared meals with them. Lately Lucien had begun to suspect there was something going on between him and Anna, although he wasn't certain. He hadn't mentioned it to Simon, for fear of sending his stress levels through the roof.

"I, also," he acknowledged. "It has been wonderful to see so much energy and enthusiasm for the sport in the children."

"Yep. These camps can often be a little too competitive, but Simon and Coach have done a great job of establishing a friendly environment. Hopefully that will continue next year."

Lucien raised a brow. "I thought it was not yet decided whether the camp would be an annual event?" It certainly hadn't been mentioned to him.

Tim waved a hand to indicate the hundred or so children ranging in age from seven to seventeen who waited in small clusters to see what the final activity of the camp would be. "After this success, how could it not?"

He had a point.

Coach blew his whistle then, and everyone quietened to hear what he had to say—and he handed over to Simon.

"Hey, everyone! We're just about done here, and I really hope you've had a great week and have picked up some tips and tricks to use over the next year and throughout your playing days." There was an enthusiastic murmur, and Lucien smiled. He'd noticed that Simon got that response even when what he was said was not at all inspiring. People just loved him.

Much like Lucien did.

"You've all worked really hard and done a great job. We've only got a little bit of time left, but we wondered if maybe you'd like to see your coaches play—" He was cut off by the roar that went up from the kids, and he laughed. "Right, so we don't have enough coaches—or enough time—for a proper match, but what about some five-a-side?" The whistles and shouts quickly approved the idea, and the camp's coaches, a veritable who's who of retired championship players from across Europe, assembled by the side of the pitch. Lucien frowned. There were only eight—two of the men had had to leave the night before due to other commitments, but because the last day was only slated to be a half-day, nobody had considered it a problem. Simon had said five-a-side, though—who would the other two players be?

His question was answered when Simon stripped off his shirt and joined the coaches. Of course—Simon and Tim hadn't actively done any coaching this week, but they were both still former professional footballers. He noticed the group was looking in their direction, and he turned to Tim. "They're waiting for you."

Tim shook his head. "Nah, mate," he said. "This knee means I can't play, not unless I want to spend a week in bed and face the possibility of more surgery."

Lucien looked back at the assembled players. Simon lifted a hand and waved. "Do they know that?" he asked. "Because it looks like they want you to join them."

"Not me, Lucien," Tim said with a laugh. "Get over there."

Shock was like a punch to the stomach. Lucien blinked. "What?"

"You know how to play, right?" Tim asked, and on autopilot, Lucien nodded. "Great. It's just a friendly kick around, so you've got nothing to worry about. Go on, they're waiting."

Forcing his legs to move, Lucien crossed the space between him and Simon, who was grinning broadly.

"Are you crazy?" he asked, and his lover laughed.

"Maybe. But mostly I'm crazy about you. Come on, Luc—football is a huge part of my life. Let me share it with you."

Despite his better judgment, Lucien smiled. How could he say no to that?

"Fine. But I don't want to hear any complaints later," he warned, and the men around him cheered.

What an amazing day.

Surprisingly, he still felt that way ten minutes later as it became increasingly obvious that he was outclassed. He'd expected that, of course—he was playing with former professional athletes, many of them championship players. It was an honor and a privilege to merely be included—and to try to keep up.

As he accepted a pass from a retired player who'd won two World Cups, he forced himself to concentrate. While he may not be in the same league as the men he was playing with, he didn't want to completely embarrass himself. Dodging a tackle—barely—he passed the ball forward.

Phew. He had a few moments now to watch his teammates and opponents play. It was a beautiful thing, but most glorious of all was his boyfriend. Simon practically glowed with joy and vitality as he dodged his opponents and kicked toward goal. His feet moved effortlessly, seemingly without conscious direction from his brain. It was just instinctive, part of him.

Lucien smiled as the ball sailed into the net and everyone on the pitch—and watching—screamed, either in happiness or disappointment. Simon ran toward him with his arms in the air, and Lucien whistled his appreciation—something his nanny had trained out of him when he was a child, but that he'd started doing again recently.

"Did you see?" Simon shouted as he got closer, his excitement akin to that of a child scoring for the first time.

"I did," Lucien told him, and then opened his arms just in time to catch Simon as he launched himself through the space between them.

Then, in front of the retired and upcoming stars of the football world, Simon Wood kissed Lucien Morel. Right on the lips.

And it was glorious.

Epilogue

Two years later

SI glanced at his watch as he hurried back to the office. Pierre Bisset had called last week and asked to meet him and Lucien for lunch today, and he was just about verging on late. Pierre was the father of Antoine Bisset, one of On the Ball's most promising kids—although at just turned eighteen, he was actually one of their graduates. Since Antoine had first applied for the program, right after it had been launched, Pierre had made a habit of occasionally coming to the office for lunch with Simon and Lucien—which he would cook and bring with him. At first it had baffled them both, but a call from Antoine had clarified. Si would never forget that call. It had been one of those rare times in the early days, not long after their first training camp, that he'd been in the office. Anna had buzzed that one of their kids wanted to talk to him, and his stomach had lurched.

"Monsieur Wood, this is Antoine Bisset," the teenager, even then extremely self-assured, had announced himself.

"Hi, Antoine," Si had replied. Antoine didn't sound upset about anything. Maybe nothing was too seriously wrong? "You can call me Simon, remember? What can I do for you?"

"I was talking to my dad today and he said he's been having lunch with you sometimes," Antoine said, his stream of French almost faster than Si's still-learning ear was able to grasp. "I just wanted to make sure that was okay."

"Of course it's okay," Si assured him. "Although, to be honest, we're not sure why he comes. He doesn't speak to us very much—it doesn't seem like he's coming for our company."

"He's not," Antoine declared bluntly. "He's bringing you lunch as a thank-you for me being in the program. It kills him that we have to take charity for me to play football, and he feels like by bringing you lunch, he's balancing the scales a bit."

Si felt like he'd been slapped in the face. "That's not necessary," he said quietly.

"I know, Simon," Antoine replied. "But it makes him feel better. Before On the Ball, he used to eat only once every few days to save money for my football. He hadn't had any new clothes or shoes in about ten years. This program has changed our lives, but his pride can't stand taking money from someone else. The only reason he does it is because he wants me to have my dream. If it makes him feel better to bring you lunch once a month, and you're okay with that, then please let him."

Si had swallowed hard and agreed. Since then, he and Lucien had made it a policy to always be available when Pierre called. They sat with him, ate whatever lunch he brought, and made awkward small talk—although that had gotten better when they'd realized they could just talk football with him.

Now, as Si pushed open the door to the building and raced up the stairs toward the office, he wondered if this would be their last lunch with Pierre. The program had officially stopped funding Antoine last month.

He entered the office and waved at Anna, who was on the phone, as he strode toward the conference room. "Sorry I'm late," he announced as he walked in and closed the door. Surprisingly, there were no covered dishes on the table. He shot a questioning glance at Lucien, who shrugged.

"You are right on time," Pierre said, then picked up his phone and tapped at the screen. Si took the seat beside Lucien, and squeezed his leg under the table. Although Pierre had enthusiastically congratulated them on their marriage the year before, they'd noticed that he was not comfortable with PDAs, and so they tried not to be too demonstrative in his presence.

"What's going on?" Si whispered. He was starving, and had been really looking forward to Pierre's lunch.

"No idea," Lucien replied. "I asked him where he'd hidden lunch, and he said we had to wait for you to arrive."

A loud ringing sound made them both jump. Pierre had clearly put his phone on speaker and called someone. He set the handset on the table with a satisfied smirk on his face.

"Finally!" someone answered the call. Si blinked. Was that Antoine? "Papa, what took so long?"

"Simon was late," Pierre told him. "But we are all here now."

"Hi, Simon, Lucien." There was glee in Antoine's voice.

"Hello, Antoine," Lucien replied while Si blinked and wondered what the heck was going on. "How are you?"

"I'm great. Guess where I am right now?"

"Do I really have to guess?" Lucien laughed.

"No, I have a better idea—switch my dad's phone over to video. He doesn't know how to do it."

Si reached for the phone before Lucien could, and tapped the necessary icon on the screen. Pierre got up and walked around the table to stand behind them as the phone switched modes and the picture appeared.

Si gasped, and grabbed for Lucien with his free hand. Antoine was grinning back at him, his phone carefully angled to include the man beside him in the camera's view—a man Si easily recognized.

"Hey, Antoine," he said, his voice shaking. Was this it? Was this going to be the moment he'd been waiting almost three years—no, almost *twenty*-three years for? "Hello, Coach."

"Hi, Simon." Antoine's smile widened even more. "Look at this." He slowly panned the camera around the room, letting them take in the club emblem, the décor that prominently featured the team colors, and the familiar faces of several club executives and a top talent agent. Lucien's hand spasmed suddenly in his. If Si had been able to tear his gaze away from the small screen in front of him, he knew he would see the same hope on his husband's face that he was feeling.

He cleared his throat. "Got some exciting news, Antoine?" There, that wasn't too bad. The words were casual, and he hadn't sounded squeaky or anything.

Antoine laughed as he came back into view, and beside him, the coach of one of France's top clubs was smiling. "The contract is right here. It's been negotiated, reviewed, and all I have to do is sign."

Si frowned suddenly, and turned to look over his shoulder. "Pierre, why aren't you there?" He remembered the day he'd signed his first professional contract. He brought both his parents, bursting with pride, and his sisters had met them afterward to celebrate.

Pierre chuckled and clapped him on the shoulder. "If I was there, who would be here with you?"

Lucien's grip on his hand tightened almost unbearably, and Si blinked back tears. "That's very kind of you," he said unsteadily, and then looked back at the phone. "And you, Antoine. Thank you for including us."

Antoine snorted, his face completely serious for the first time since the camera had gone on. "No. I was one month away from dropping football when you launched On the Ball. I'd applied for every damn scholarship out there, but competition was fierce, and there was no way I was letting my dad go without anymore just so I could play. I was going to give it one more month, because that was when the last two scholarships I'd applied for would be announced, and then that was it. I was going to accept the fact that I'd just be playing for fun or in a weekend neighborhood league. Then suddenly one day I'm at school and at lunch everyone starts talking about this new scholarship program. One of *my idols*, one of the men I'd always admired and aspired to be like, was starting a program so kids could play football. I skipped my classes that afternoon so I could fill out the application, and since then I've never looked back. On the Ball changed my life. Simon and Lucien, *you* changed my life. And now, thanks to you, it's going to change again. Hold this, Victor." He thrust the phone toward the talent agent, who took it and kept the camera focused on him. Antoine picked up the pen... and signed the contract.

Simon didn't even try to hold back the tears that streamed down his face.

While everyone in that room congratulated Antoine, Simon turned his head and buried his face against Lucien's shoulder. They'd done it. They'd actually done it. One of their kids was now a professional footballer.

"Simon," Lucien said, moving his shoulder sharply. Si lifted his head, and Lucien nodded toward the phone. In the background, the congratulations continued, but the screen was centered on Victor Caron's face.

Si wiped his cheeks, not even a little bit ashamed of his tears. He'd *earned* them. "Hello, Victor."

The agent, a man known for being scrupulously honest and fair with his clients but utterly ruthless in negotiations, smiled. "Get used to this feeling. I'm working with two of your other kids at the moment, and colleagues of mine in Germany and Belgium tell me they too are in talks with On the Ball players. Those are only the ones I know about. You'll have cause for celebration again soon."

While Si was digesting that, Antoine snatched the phone away from Victor. "Right, we're all going out to lunch to celebrate. Papa, did you organize the car?"

"It should be outside right now," Pierre assured him. "We will meet you at the restaurant."

Si's stomach sank. "I have an appointment in an hour," he said regretfully, glancing at Lucien, whose face reflected the same dismay.

"No, you don't," Antoine told him. "Anna canceled it. You too, Lucien. By the way, your assistant is scary."

Si blinked. "Anna knew? And Paul?"

Antoine shrugged. "I had to make sure you were free to celebrate with us. They were both pretty excited—I didn't think they'd be able to keep it a secret."

Pierre ushered Si and Lucien out of their seats. "Of course they kept it a secret. They knew Simon and Lucien deserved this surprise."

As they walked through the main office to the sound of Anna's and Michel's cheers, Si thought back to that day three years ago when he'd waited, in a building not far away, for a meeting with Édouard Morel. He'd been nervous then, more nervous than he had ever been as a championship professional footballer. A phase of his life had been over, and he'd been waiting to find out if his dreams for the next phase could possibly come true. He'd known the meeting had the power to change his life, but... could he ever have expected this? The fulfillment of a dream, a home in a new country, new friends, meeting the love of his life, coming out to the world... his husband.

He slid his arm around Lucien's waist and leaned into him while they waited for the elevator. Pierre looked away, and Si smiled indulgently at him. Lucien bent his head and rested it against his.

"I love you," he whispered.

Si grinned. Nothing could ever make those words less magical. He turned his head and caught Lucien's lips with his. "I love you."

Life was good.

Coming in February 2019

DREAMSPUN DESIRES

Dreamspun Desires #75
Rebuild My Heart by Ariel Tachna

A love built to last.

When Derek Jackson is hired to renovate the LGBT bookstore that's also Owen Hensley's home, opposites attract. Derek is a big burly blue-collar guy, about ten years older than slight, sweet, shy, and bookish Owen. As they spend time together, it becomes clear that each handsome outside leads to a beautiful interior. Far from the timid twink he appears, Owen has a rock-solid foundation that helped him put himself through college and start his own business. Behind Derek's strong façade waits a tender heart that's been battered by a rough family past—something Owen understands.

When Owen's runaway nephew lands on his doorstep, it throws a wrench in their plans. Derek can't ask Owen to choose, but he doesn't think he can take second place with his lover the way he always has with his family. Can they find a way to keep their romance standing?

Dreamspun Desires #76
My Fair Brady by K.C. Wells

A spur of the moment invitation changes two lives.

Jordan Wolf's company runs like a well-oiled machine. At least until his PA, Brady Donovan, comes down with the flu and takes sick leave. Then Jordan discovers what a treasure Brady is and who really keeps his business—and Jordan in particular— moving like clockwork. So when Jordan needs a plus-one, Brady seems the obvious choice to accompany him. After a major shopping trip to get Brady looking the part, however…. Wow.

Brady has a whole new wardrobe, and now his boss is whisking him away for a weekend party. Something is going on, something Brady never expected: Jordan is looking at him like he's never seen him before, electrifying Brady's long-hidden desires.

But can the romantic magic last when the weekend is over and it's back to reality?